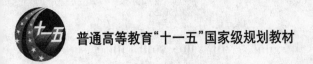

普通高等教育"十一五"国家级规划教材　　全国成人高等教育规划教材

现代

[第二版]

英语教程

A MODERN ENGLISH COURSE

⊙主编：楼光庆
编者：宫东风　王丽萍

2
教学指导与练习

外语教学与研究出版社
FOREIGN LANGUAGE TEACHING AND RESEARCH PRESS
北京　BEIJING

图书在版编目(CIP)数据

现代英语教程教学指导与练习. 2／楼光庆主编 .— 2 版 .— 北京：外语教学与研究出版社，2008.11

ISBN 978 - 7 - 5600 - 7949 - 3

Ⅰ. 现… Ⅱ. 楼… Ⅲ. 英语—成人教育：高等教育—教学参考资料 Ⅳ. H31

中国版本图书馆 CIP 数据核字 (2008) 第 174637 号

出　版　人：于春迟
项目负责：赵东岳　高淑芬
责任编辑：高淑芬
执行编辑：李　萍
装帧设计：刘　冬
出版发行：外语教学与研究出版社
社　　址：北京市西三环北路 19 号 (100089)
网　　址：http://www.fltrp.com
印　　刷：北京京科印刷有限公司
开　　本：787×1092　1/16
印　　张：9.5
版　　次：2008 年 11 月第 1 版　2008 年 11 月第 1 次印刷
书　　号：ISBN 978 - 7 - 5600 - 7949 - 3
定　　价：15.90 元

＊　　＊　　＊

编委会成员

主　编：楼光庆

编　委：屠　蓓　马荣华

　　　　曾添桂　王丽萍

　　　　宫东风　吴　群

　　　　冯国华　王琛明

前 言（第二版）

　　《现代英语教程》是一套专门为中国成人高等教育学生编写的英语教材。教材的编写遵照"综合法"（Method Synergistics）的教学理论，采用博采众长，兼收并蓄的原则，强调基本功的训练，要求学生精练、勤练、苦练，顺利通过英语学习的入门关，帮助非英语专业成人本科学生通过申请学士学位所必需的英语统一考试。

　　《现代英语教程》是在国家教育部、北京市教育委员会有关领导的支持和推动下，以及兄弟院校同仁们的鼓励下问世的。1999 年起在北京市成人高校试用，2000 年国家教育部在全国推广使用。学校使用后反应教学效果显著，学生实际应用英语的能力得到普遍提高，因而受到广大师生们的好评。《现代英语教程》先后被评为教育部"全国成人高等教育规划教材"（2001 年），"普通高等教育'十五'国家级规划教材"（2003 年），"普通高等教育'十一五'国家级规划教材"（2006 年）。

　　"成人，业余，终身化"是本套教材的最大特点。因而，贯穿始终的编写原则是要培养学生的自学能力，帮助学生掌握学好英语的方法。学生不仅要正确理解，还要善于应用；不仅要会听说，还要会读写。

　　为适应我国成人高等教育发展的需要，在获得了各方面好评和认可的情况下，根据收集到的反馈意见和有关专家的建议及教学目标要求，我们对该套教材进行了进一步修订。在保持教材原有优点的同时，新版大幅度地丰富了内容，增加了信息量和练习；语法项目安排更加完整、系统；各单元都增加了听力练习。部分课文内容进行了更新，特别是第三至六级，跨度更趋循序渐进。教师用书的每单元增加了背景知识及课文详解，这样会更利于学生能力的训练，也更便于教师们使用。原教材主体为一、二、三级。为使教材更加科学、合理，同时也根据社会需求，这次，我们将《现代英语教程》（第二版）修订改编成六级，其中一至三级供专科学生使用，四至六级供专升本学生使用。

　　《现代英语教程》（第二版）配有多媒体光盘，从而构成了一套名副其实的含纸介教材，录音带和光盘的全新立体化教材。

　　在教材的修订过程中，我们得到了外语教学与研究出版社的大力支持和通力协作，特别是高等英语教育出版分社常小玲社长，项目负责人赵东岳编辑，多媒体部倪睿编辑。他们自始至终参与了策划工作，提供了大量反馈信息，并承担了繁重的编辑任务。在此，我们向他们致以诚挚的谢意。

　　由于水平有限，不当之处，在所难免，衷心希望广大教师和学生批评指正，以便我们进一步改进和完善此套教材。

编者

2007 年 8 月

编写说明（第二版）

一、编写依据

《现代英语教程》（第二版）的编写依据为：

1.《全国成人高等教育英语课程教学基本要求（非英语专业专科用）》；

2.《全国成人高等教育英语专业（专科）英语教学基本要求》；

3.《成人高等教育学士学位英语水平考试大纲（非英语专业）》；

4.《大学英语课程教学要求》；

5.《北京地区成人本科学士学位英语统一考试考务管理工作手册（2006版）》；

6.近年来使用本套教材的教师、学生的反馈意见。

二、教学对象

本教材的教学对象是成人高等教育各专业的学生。学习形式以非全日制，在职业余学习为主。学生入学时应掌握基本的语音和语法知识，认知单词1,200个。在听、说、读、写等方面受过初步的训练。本教材也适合同等英语水平的高职高专学生使用。

三、教学要求

通过本教材的教学，学生应掌握一定的英语基础知识和技能，具有阅读和翻译一般的英语业务资料，进行简单听、说、写的语言应用能力，为今后继续提高英语交际能力打下基础。

通过本教材的教学，学生应能认知英语单词3,000个左右（包括入学时要求掌握的1,200个单词），对其中1,000个左右的单词能正确拼写、英汉互译，并能熟练掌握其中200个左右常用词组的基本词义和用法；掌握基本的阅读技能；能运用国际音标拼读单词，朗读时语音语调基本正确；掌握基本语法规则，并能解决阅读与翻译中的一般语法问题；能运用学到的语言知识，写出正确的句子和简单书信等应用文；能听懂没有生词的会话或简单短文；能用英语进行简单日常会话；能借助词典把一般难度的英文文章译成汉语。

四、教程说明

1.课程教学对象为高等应用型人才。我们既要向学生传授必要的语言系统知识，更要培养他们实际应用语言的能力；注意素质教育，培养学生的分析能力和文化差异包容意识。

2. 充分考虑成人学生学习外语的特点，要鼓励自学，要贯彻"终身化"教育思想。要充分利用现代化教学手段，处理好传授与练习、上课与自学、学生主动性与教师主导作用等关系。

3. 英语课程总课时为 216 学时。本教材所需课时为 160－180 学时。其余课时作为与本专业有关的英语学习使用。

4. 重点培养学生的阅读技能，但也要进行必要的听、说、写及翻译技能的训练。

5. 所选用的文章都为难度适当的原文，一般不进行改写。为达到教学目的而必须进行改写时则注意作品的完整性，保持行文流畅，英语地道。

6. 题材多样化（50% 文科类，50% 非文科类），富有时代感，偏重实用性。

7. 选材、练习、举例等都注意了"得体性"（Appropriateness）。

8. 练习超越传统的公共外语练习形式——单纯机械的多项选择，而采取让学生自己动手动脑才能完成的综合练习方式。

五、教程内容

本教程第一至三级为专科教材，《英语语音》为基础教材，帮助学生进行复习和整理，第四至六级为专升本教材。

《英语语音》帮助学生进一步学习国际音标及基本语音语调，使学生达到能够熟练运用国际音标拼读单词，辨别音素及重音，能运用正确的语调进行交流的目的。

第一至三级的具体安排如下：

1. 每册为 10 个单元。每单元建议授课学时为 6 学时（3 学时×2 周）。

2. 每单元包括课文（Text）和阅读（Reading）。课文较短，重点讲解语言点，进行篇章分析。阅读部分的文章稍长，主要培养阅读能力，文中逐步出现认知词汇，科普（50%）与人文社会科学（50%）内容与课文相近。

3. 每单元对学生明确提出预习要求，对课文大意以及关键词组提出问题，要求学生解答，逐步培养学生使用工具书和独立解决问题的能力。

4. 在每篇课文中根据内容、语言特点设定重点段，要求学生熟读，背诵。

5. 每单元对课文的语言难点、时代背景做中文注释。

6. 语法项目列表直线排列（见附表），并贯穿各册书。针对中国学生学习英语的难点，突出重点，滚动式出现，前后呼应。

7. 写作练习（Writing）从第二级开始（见附表），逐步介绍句子、段落等。

8. 口语练习（Speaking）和听力练习（Listening）贯穿全套教材，提供日常生活的简单会话及听力练习材料。

9. 每单元的练习涉及：理解、词汇、语法、写作、口语、听力等，强调精练、勤练、多练，便于自学巩固。

10. 为便于学生自学及教师的教学工作，每级配有《教学指导与练习》，内容包括较详尽的背景知识（Background Knowledge）、课文详解（Detailed Notes

to the Text）、练习答案（Key to Exercises）、听写练习（Dictation）、补充阅读（Supplementary Reading），课文参考译文（Chinese Translation）及三份百分制的测试卷。听写练习也可供教师在课堂上做听力练习用，测试卷供教师选用。

　　《现代英语教程》（第二版）主编为北京外国语大学楼光庆教授。《英语语音》编者为北京外国语大学屠蓓教授。第一级编者为北京外国语大学马荣华副教授、北京师范大学曾添桂副教授。第二级编者为首都师范大学王丽萍副教授、北京信息职业技术学院宫东风副教授。第三级编者为北京师范大学曾添桂副教授、北京外国语大学马荣华副教授。

编者
2007 年 8 月

附表

教程内容
（Books 1–3）

《现代英语教程》（第二版）

Book 1	Book 2	Book 3
课文（Text） 语法（Grammar） 阅读（Reading） 听力（Listening） 口语（Speaking） 附录： 1. 不规则动词表 2. 英语构词法简介	课文（Text） 语法（Grammar） 写作（Writing） 阅读（Reading） 听力（Listening） 口语（Speaking）	课文（Text） 语法（Grammar） 写作（Writing） 阅读（Reading） 听力（Listening） 口语（Speaking）

语法（Grammar）

Book 1	Book 2	Book 3
Unit 1 现在一般时（1） (Present Simple Tense I)	Unit 1 名词（1） (Nouns I)	Unit 1 过去进行时 (Past Progressive Tense)
Unit 2 现在一般时（2） (Present Simple Tense II)	Unit 2 名词（2） (Nouns II)	Unit 2 过去完成时 (Past Perfect Tense)
Unit 3 现在进行时（1） (Present Progressive Tense I)	Unit 3 冠词 (Articles)	Unit 3 被动语态 (Passive Voice)
Unit 4 现在进行时（2） (Present Progressive Tense II)	Unit 4 代词 (Pronouns)	Unit 4 虚拟语气 (Subjunctive Mood)
Unit 5 将来一般时（1） (Future Simple Tense I)	Unit 5 数词 (Numerals)	Unit 5 非限定动词（1） (Non-Finite Verb Forms I)
Unit 6 将来一般时（2） (Future Simple Tense II)	Unit 6 介词 (Prepositions)	Unit 6 非限定动词（1） (Non-Finite Verb Forms II)
Unit 7 过去一般时（1） (Past Simple Tense I)	Unit 7 形容词和副词（1） (Adjectives & Adverbs I)	Unit 7 宾语从句 (Object Clause)

（待续）

（续上表）

Book 1	Book 2	Book 3
Unit 8 过去一般时（2） (Past Simple Tense II)	Unit 8 形容词和副词（2） (Adjectives & Adverbs II)	Unit 8 直接引语和间接引语 (Direct Speech and Indirect Speech)
Unit 9 现在完成时（1） (Present Perfect Tense I)	Unit 9 情态动词（1） (Modal Verbs I)	Unit 9 引导词 It 引导的结构 ("It" Structure)
Unit 10 现在完成时（2） (Present Perfect Tense II)	Unit 10 情态动词（2） (Modal Verbs II)	Unit 10 词序倒装 (Inverted Word Order)

写作（Writing）

Book 1	Book 2	Book 3
无（No Writing）	Unit 1 句子（1） (Sentences I)	Unit 1 段落中的主题句 (Topic Sentence of a Paragraph)
	Unit 2 句子（2） (Sentences II)	Unit 2 段落中的发展句、转折句和结论句 (Paragraph Developer, Transitional Sentence & Conclusion)
	Unit 3 状语从句（1） (Adverbial Clauses I)	Unit 3 段落的统一性 (Paragraph Unity)
	Unit 4 状语从句（2） (Adverbial Clauses II)	Unit 4 段落的连贯性（1） (Paragraph Coherence I)
	Unit 5 状语从句（3） (Adverbial Clauses III)	Unit 5 段落的连贯性（2） (Paragraph Coherence II)
	Unit 6 状语从句（4） (Adverbial Clauses IV)	Unit 6 列举法与举例法 (List & Example Paragraphs)
	Unit 7 名词从句（1） (Nominal Clauses I)	Unit 7 时间顺序段落 (Chronological Paragraphs) 空间顺序段落 (Spatial Paragraphs)
	Unit 8 名词从句（2） (Nominal Clauses II)	

（待续）

(续上表)

Book 1	Book 2	Book 3
无（No Writing）	Unit 9 定语从句（1） (Attributive Clauses I) Unit 10 定语从句（2） (Attributive Clauses II)	过程顺序段落 (Process Paragraphs) Unit 8 分类法与定义法 (Classification & Definition) Unit 9 比较法与对比法 (Comparison & Contrast) Unit 10 因果法 (Cause & Effect)

《教学指导与练习》

Book 1	Book 2	Book 3
一、背景资料 （Background Knowledge） 二、课文详解 （Detailed Notes to the Text） 三、参考答案 （Key to Exercises） 四、课文参考译文 （Chinese Translation） 五、测试卷及答案 （English Proficiency Tests）	一、背景资料 （Background Knowledge） 二、课文详解 （Detailed Notes to the Text） 三、参考答案 （Key to Exercises） 四、课文参考译文 （Chinese Translation） 五、测试卷及答案 （English Proficiency Tests）	一、背景资料 （Background Knowledge） 二、课文详解 （Detailed Notes to the Text） 三、参考答案 （Key to Exercises） 四、课文参考译文 （Chinese Translation） 五、测试卷及答案 （English Proficiency Tests）

CONTENTS

目录

1

UNIT 1 *The Sea*

Background Knowledge（背景知识）

1961 年 4 月 12 日，世界第一名航天员、苏联宇航员加加林驾驶"东方 1 号"宇宙飞船，完成了人类历史上首次太空飞行，使人类第一次从太空观察到了自己居住的地球，并提出了地球是一个水球的论点。因为他观察到的地球表面海洋面积远远大于陆地面积。根据多年的科学研究，地球表面总面积为 5.1 亿平方公里；海洋占 70.8%，面积是 3.61 亿平方公里；陆地占 29.2%，面积为 1.49 亿平方公里。

地球上的海洋是相互连通的，有太平洋、大西洋、印度洋、北冰洋四大洋。海是洋的边缘部分，在大陆之间或紧临大陆边缘，水深较浅，受陆地影响显著。全世界有 54 个海。

根据海洋测量资料，海底的基本轮廓是这样的：海水与陆地相接的地方，叫海岸带。全世界有 60% 的人居住在沿海地区，这里是经济发达、人们建设活动最频繁的地区。从海岸向海，是坡度不大，比较平坦的海底，叫大陆架。再向外，是一个相当陡峭的大斜坡，从水深 200 米直降到 3000 米，这个斜坡叫大陆坡。从大陆坡往下便是广阔的大洋底部了。大洋底深 4000～5000 米，有规模宏大的海底山脉、海底高原、深海平原和深海盆地。另外还有一些洋底火山、珊瑚礁等。

海洋蕴藏着丰富的矿产资源。在浅海平原，有丰富的海底石油、天然气和煤层；在大洋底、海底山脉、海底高原上，蕴藏着丰富的铁、锰、铜等矿物；在深海平原的红黏土中含有丰富的铀。仅太平洋底的一个区域，海底的镍、铜、钴、锰、磷等矿产资源的储量就达 1500 亿吨。

海洋是生物资源宝库。据生物学家统计，海洋中约有 20 万种生物，其中已知鱼类约 1.9 万种，甲壳类约 2 万种。许多海洋生物具有开发利用价值，为人类提供了丰富的食物和其他资源。世界海洋浮游植物产量 5000 亿吨，折合成鱼类年生产量约 6 亿吨。假如以 50% 的资源量为可捕量，则世界海洋中鱼类可捕量约 3 亿吨。

浩瀚的大海有取之不尽，用之不竭的能源。它既不同于海底所储存的煤、石油、天然气等海底能源资源，也不同于溶于水中的铀、镁、锂、重水等化学能源资源。它有自己独特的方式与形态，即用潮汐、波浪、海流、温度差、盐度差等方式表达的动能、势能、热能、物理化学能等能源。直接地说就是潮汐能、波浪能、海水温差能、海流能及盐度差能等。这是一种"再生性能源"，永远不会枯竭，也不会造成任何污染。

Detailed Notes to the Text（课文详解）

1. It looks beautiful on a fine sunny day...

look 作系动词时表示"看起来"，后面可以跟：

1) 形容词。例如：

She looked very tired, but she was still cheerful.

她看上去很疲倦但很快活。

He looked nervous and apologetic.

他看上去紧张并带有歉意。

What's wrong with you? You are looking green.

你怎么啦？看上去脸色发青。

2) 过去分词。例如：

She looked embarrassed.

她看起来有些尴尬。

He looked startled when his nephew came in.

他侄子进来的时候他简直惊呆了。

He turned to me looking very concerned and troubled.

他转过来朝着我，一脸忧虑和困惑。

3) 名词。例如：

Hayward looked a perfect fool.

西沃德看上去是个十足的傻瓜。

He looks a nice, reliable man.

他看起来是个和善、可靠的人。

It looks a lovely house.

真是一所漂亮的房子。

4) 介词短语等。例如：

He looked in splendid health.

他看上去非常健康。

The weather does not look like clearing up.

天气不像会放晴的样子。

She looked about fourteen.

她看上去大约 14 岁。

You looked as if you didn't care.

你看起来好像不在乎。

2. 1) In the world there is more sea than land.

   2) Some parts of the sea are more salty than other parts.

   more 在以上两句中分别构成形容词和副词的比较级。例如：

   His illness was (much) more serious than the doctor first thought.

   他的病比医生最初想象的要严重（得多）。

   Sheila's behavior became more than ever strange.

   希拉的行为变得比任何时候都奇怪。

   She was the more promising employee of the two.

   两个员工中她更有前途。

3. The sea covers more than two thirds of the earth.

   cover 在此表示 "面积有多大"。例如：

   The city covered ten square kilometers.

   这个城市面积是 10 平方公里。

   Its European territory covered about 2,000,000 square miles.

   它的欧洲部分面积大约是 200 万平方英里。

   cover 作为动词还表示：

   1) 报道（有关……的消息）。例如：

      The best reporters were sent to cover the war.

      最好的记者们被派去报道这场战争。

      This paper covers sports thoroughly.

      这份报纸全面报道体育新闻。

      She will cover the trial for the paper.

      她将为这份报纸报道有关审判的消息。

   2) 谈到，涉及，包含。例如：

      The discussion covered a wide range of subjects.

      讨论涉及到了广泛的主题。

      The doctor's talk covered the history of medicine from Roman times to present day.

      医生谈到了从罗马时代至今的医学历史。

      What is your opinion of the amount of material covered?

      对刚才看过的这部分材料你有什么看法？

   3) 走完（一段路程），够付（费用），看完（多少页书）。例如：

      They covered twelve miles yesterday.

      昨天他们走了 12 英里路。

I wonder how I'll cover all these expenses.

我真不知道怎么才能付清这些费用。

How many pages have you covered?

你读完了多少页？

4. 1) But in some places the depth of the sea is very great.

2) No sunlight can reach the depths of the sea...

depth 第一组例句中表示"深度（不可数）"，在第 2 组例句中表示"深处（多作复数）"。例如：

1）What is the depth of the lake?

这湖有多深？

The snow is three feet in depth.

雪有三英尺深。

The book shows the author's depth of learning.

书的内容显示了作者深厚的学术功底。

2）Coal miners have to work in the depths of the earth.

矿工必须在很深的地底下工作。

in the depths of the ocean 海底

in the depths of winter 隆冬

in the depths of one's heart 心底

in the depths of despair 绝望

5. Swimmers cannot sink in it!

sink（sank, sunk）在此表示"沉没"。例如：

The ocean liner *Titanic* sank in 1912.

"泰坦尼克号"远洋客轮于 1912 年沉没。

Wood does not sink in water; it floats.

木头在水中不会沉下去，只会浮起来。

His foot sank in the mud.

他的脚陷在了泥中。

sink 还可表示：

1）下降，减弱，变得虚弱。例如：

Their standard of living steadily sank down.

他们的生活水平不断地下降。

His reputation has sunk in our opinion.

在我们眼中他的威望下降了。

The patient's health seemed to sink overnight.

病人的健康似乎一夜之间就恶化了。

He's sinking fast and won't live much longer.

他日渐虚弱，不会活得太久了。

2) 使沉没，击（凿）沉。例如：

A small leak will sink a great ship.

小患不治成大灾 / 千里之堤，溃于蚁穴。

The submarine sank two vessels on her first voyage.

潜水艇第一次出航就击沉两艘船。

The torpedo sank the battleship immediately.

鱼雷片刻之间就把战舰击沉了。

6. In most parts of the sea, there are a lot of fishes and plants.

plants 作为名词表示"植物"，为可数名词。例如：

All plants need water and light.

植物都离不了水和光。

fish 为可数名词，但复数一般多作 fish。例如：

I caught a fish.

我抓到了一条鱼。

Could you catch those fish?

你能抓到那些鱼吗？

表示不同种类的鱼时才用 fishes。例如：

There were fishes of many hues and sizes.

有不同颜色和大小的鱼（类）。

We'll go and look at the fishes in the aquarium.

我们要去海洋馆看各种鱼。

7. They hope to find new resources for mankind.

resources（复数形式）表示"资源"。例如：

This country is rich in natural resources.

这个国家自然资源丰富。

We must exploit the natural resources of our country.

我们必须开发我国的自然资源。

She is the manager of Human Resources Department.

她是人力资源部经理。

有时可作单数。例如：

Oil is an important natural resource.

石油是一种重要的自然资源。

习惯用法 leave someone to his own resources，意为"让某人自己去想办法消磨时间"。例如：

Leave him to his own resources.

让他自己去想办法消磨时间吧！

After they had finished interviewing her, they left her to her own resources.

面试完她以后，他们就不去管她了。

▶ Supplementary Grammar（语法补充材料）

1. 名词的复数形式，一般是在单数形式后面加 -s 或 -es。现将构成方法与读音规则列表如下：

构成方法	读音	例词
在词末加 -s	1. 在清辅音后读作 /s/ 2. 在浊辅音和元音后读作 /z/	1. desk — desks /desks/ 书桌 　 map — maps /mæps/ 地图 　 boat — boats /bəʊts/ 船 　 lake — lakes /leɪks/ 湖 2. field — fields /fiːldz/ 田地 　 dog — dogs /dɒgz/ 狗 　 machine — machines /məˈʃiːnz/ 机器 　 sea — seas /siːz/ 海
1. 在以 /s/, /z/, /ʃ/, /ʒ/, /tʃ/, /dʒ/ 等音结尾的名词之后加 -es 2. 如词末为 e，只加 -s	-(e)s 读作 /ɪz/	1. class — classes /ˈklɑːsɪz/ 班级 　 buzz — buzzes /ˈbʌzɪz/ 嗡嗡声 　 dish — dishes /ˈdɪʃɪz/ 盘子 　 church — churches /ˈtʃəːtʃɪz/ 教堂 2. horse — horses /ˈhɔːsɪz/ 马 　 bridge — bridges /ˈbrɪdʒɪz/ 桥 　 page — pages /ˈpeɪdʒɪz/ 页 　 mirage — mirages /ˈmɪrɑːʒɪz/ 幻景
如词末为 -f 或 -fe，则一般变为 v，再加 -es	-ves 读作 /vz/	leaf — leaves /liːvz/ 叶 thief — thieves /θiːvz/ 小偷 shelf — shelves /ʃelvz/ 搁板 knife — knives /naɪvz/ 小刀

（待续）

（续上表）

构成方法	读音	例词
如词末为辅音加 y，则变 y 为 i，再加 -es	-ies 读作 /ɪz/	party — parties /ˈpɑːtɪz/ 聚会 factory — factories /ˈfæktrɪz/ 工厂 family — families /ˈfæmɪlɪz/ 家庭 university — universities /ˌjuːnɪˈvɜːsətɪz/ 大学
如词末为元音加 y，则加 -s	-s 读作 /z/	boy — boys /bɔɪz/ 男孩 ray — rays /reɪz/ 光线 toy — toys /tɔɪz/ 玩具 guy — guys /gaɪz/ 哥儿们
如词末为辅音加 o，一般加 -es	-es 读作 /z/	hero — heroes /ˈhɪərəʊz/ 英雄 echo — echoes /ˈekəʊz/ 回声 potato — potatoes /pəˈteɪtəʊz/ 土豆 tomato — tomatoes /təˈmɑːtəʊz/ 西红柿
如词末为 -th，则加 -s	1. 在长元音及双元音后，-ths 读作 /ðz/ 2. 在短元音或辅音后，-ths 读作 /θs/	1. bath — baths /bɑːðz/ 浴 youth — youths /juːðz/ 青年 path — paths /pɑːðz/ 小径 mouth — mouths /maʊðz/ 嘴 2. moth — moths /mɒθs/ 蛾 month — months /mʌnθs/ 月份

上述情况有不少例外。

1) 不少以 -o 结尾的外来词，变为复数形式时只加 -s。例如：

piano — pianos 钢琴　　　　　　　　radio — radios 收音机

dynamo — dynamos 发电机　　　　　studio — studios 画室

2) 请注意下述有关字母、数字、缩写词以及引语的复数形式：

the a's 字母 a　　　　　　　　　　the s'es 字母 s

four 4's 4 个 4　　　　　　　　　　in the 1980's 20 世纪 80 年代

例如：

（1）He always speaks with the utmost politeness, full of *maam's* and *if I may ask a question's*.

他的言谈总是彬彬有礼，频频使用"夫人"和"假如我可以提一个问题的话"这类客套话。

（2）Don't stand there with your *ayes* and *sures*.

你不要站在那里光说："是！一定！"

2. 名词的不规则复数形式

英语里有一些名词的复数形式不是以词尾加 -s 或 -es 构成。这些复数形式称为不规则复数形式。它们的构成方法主要如下表：

构成方法	例词
变内部元音	foot /fut/ — feet /fiːt/ 脚 man /mæn/ — men /men/ 男人 mouse /maʊs/ — mice /maɪs/ 鼠 tooth /tuːθ/ — teeth /tiːθ/ 齿 woman /ˈwʊmən/ — women /ˈwɪmɪn/ 女人
词末加 -en（有时同时变化词中的元音）	child /tʃaɪld/ — children /ˈtʃɪldrən/ 小孩 ox /ɒks/ — oxen /ˈɒksən/ 公牛
形式不变（通形名词）	deer /dɪə/ — deer 鹿 fish /fɪʃ/ — fish 鱼 means /miːnz/ — means 方法 series /ˈsɪəriːz/ — series 系列 sheep /ʃiːp/ — sheep 羊 Chinese- /tʃaɪˈniːz/ — Chinese 中国人
某些外来词有特殊的变化	criterion /kraɪˈtɪərɪən/ — criteria /kraɪˈtɪərɪə/ 标准 phenomenon /fɪˈnɒmɪnən/ — phenomena /fɪˈnɒmɪnə/ 现象 syllabus /ˈsɪləbəs/ — syllabi /ˈsɪləbaɪ/ 课程提纲

直接从汉语译音的名词（斜体）一般无复数形式。例如：

three *li*	三里	20 *dan*	20 担
fifty *mu*	50 亩	six *yuan*	六元

Key to Exercises（参考答案）

1. 1) It looks beautiful.

   2) It can be very rough.

   3) Yes, there is.

   4) No, it isn't. Some parts of it are very shallow.

   5) It is nearly 11 kilometers deep.

   6) It is very salty. Swimmers cannot sink in it! Fish cannot live in the Dead Sea. It's a strange sea.

   7) Because no sunlight can reach the depths of the sea, so it is completely dark.

8) Strange fish live there. Some are blind. Some have their own lights. Some have great jaws.

9) The water near the top of the sea is warmer.

10) They hope to find new resources for mankind.

2. 1) looked   2) knows   3) looking   4) carry   5) take

   6) carried   7) bring   8) carries   9) take   10) take, bring

3. 1) C   2) C   3) B   4) B   5) A

   6) C   7) C   8) C   9) C   10) D

   11) D   12) C   13) C   14) A   15) B

   16) A   17) D   18) C   19) D   20) D

4. A. 1) Tom but not his sister is studying English.

     2) Neither John nor Mary is a student.

     3) I didn't meet either Jane or her husband. / I met neither Jane nor her husband.

     4) They sang and danced all night.

   B. 1) After we were informed the flight would be delayed, we made other arrangements.

     2) Unless it is changed, this law will make life difficult for farmers.

     3) Although they debated for hours, no decision was made.

     4) The train which is arriving at Platform 8 is the 17:50 express from Beijing.

     5) We are grateful to you that you have given us so much help.

   C. 1) He walked out of the room and he slammed the door behind him.

     2) I threw the ball to Tom, and he threw it to Ann.

     3) I was caught in the heavy rain, and it made me ill.

     4) I met Mary, and then she invited me to a party.

     5) Milk must be kept in a cool place, or else it will go sour.

5. A. 1) Land covers only one third of the earth.

     2) Our new classroom building is 25 metres high.

     3) Scientists are making a study of the ocean issues.

     4) *Titanic* sank because of the iceberg.

     5) Have you ever swum in the sea?

     6) It is getting colder and colder.

     7) The Yangtze River is the longest river in China.

8) He plays the violin better than Mary.

9) The summer in Wuhan is much hotter than it is in Beijing.

10) Sound travels much more slowly than light.

B. 1) 世界上海洋的面积大于陆地。

2) 世界上最高的山峰也仅有大约 9000 米高。

3) 某些地方的海水要比其他地方的海水咸。

4) 它们用其巨大无比的嘴吞食比自身还要大的鱼。

5) 随着潜水员下沉，海水变得越来越冷。

6) 玛丽汉语讲得比约翰好。

7) 这是课文中最难的句子。

8) 在我们班，她游泳游得最好。

9) 他是我们三个人中年龄最小的。

10) 她是女生中学习最用功的。

6. 1) B   2) C   3) D   4) D   5) A

   6) C   7) C   8) A   9) C   10) B

Reading:

1. 1) A   2) A   3) C   4) D   5) C

2. 1) T   2) F   3) F   4) T   5) T

Listening:

1. W: Would you like to listen to the latest popular music record?

   M: Sure, it's got one of my favourite songs on it.

   Q: What are the man and the woman doing?

2. M: Linda, could you type the report again?

   W: Certainly, I'll do it right away.

   Q: What will the woman do?

3. M: It is certain that the manager will agree with us on the proposal.

   W: I don't think so.

   Q: What's the woman's opinion about the proposal?

4. W: Helen's done very well , hasn't she?

  M: I'm afraid not. She said she didn't finish writing the composition.

  Q: What did Helen take part in?

5. M: Is Jane bringing some drinks this evening?

  W: I think she is, but I am not quite sure.

  Q: Where is Jane going this evening?

Key:

1. C	2. B	3. B	4. D	5. C

Dictation:

Ladies and Gentlemen,

Welcome to London International Language Centre. We teach English for both practical and business purposes. Our teachers are well experienced. They use modern teaching methods and facilities to help students improve their English. You may go to Room 115 to register for our language courses.

In addition to formal classroom teaching, we offer our students a lot of other activities, including movies, English Corners, discussions and outings. All those activities are designed to help students improve their English language skills.

Our English Club opens from 9 a.m. to 9 p.m. every day. Members are free to use all the facilities of the club. All you have to do is to apply for a card.

Thank you.

Chinese Translation (课文参考译文)

大海

关于海，你知道些什么？你也许曾经看见过大海。一些人还在大海里游过泳。在阳光明媚的日子，大海看起来非常美丽。而在大风中，大海会变得波涛汹涌。关于大海，我们还知道些什么呢？

当然，海是浩瀚的。世界上海洋的面积大于陆地。海洋面积超过了地球表面的三分之二。

在一些地方，海非常深。不过并非处处都深，也有很浅的地方。在某些地方，大海深不可测。如在太平洋某处，大海深度竟达1万1千米！设想一下！世界上最高的山峰也仅有大约9000米高！

如果你在海里游过泳，你就知道海水是咸的。河水将盐从陆地带入大海。某些地方的海水要比其他地方的海水咸。你知道阿拉伯半岛的死海吗？它的水非常咸。在死海里游泳是不会下沉的！鱼无法在死海里生存。死海真是一个奇异的海。

在海洋的大多数地方，有许多鱼和植物。一些靠近海表生存；另一些则生存在海洋的深处。阳光无法照射到海洋的深处，因此那里一片黑暗。许多稀奇古怪的鱼类生活在那里：有些鱼没有视觉，有些鱼自己会发光，有些鱼有巨大的颚，它们用其巨大无比的嘴吞食比自身还要大的鱼。

海水非常冷。深海潜水者对这一点很了解。在海洋的上层，海水或许是温暖的。随着潜水员下沉，海水变得越来越冷。

目前，许多科学家正在进行一项关于海洋动植物的研究。他们希望为人类找到新的资源。

UNIT 2

A Letter to a Teacher

Background Knowledge（背景知识）

　　课文中提到的皮尔逊学院（Pearson College），位于加拿大不列颠哥伦比亚省维多利亚市郊，是建立于全球五大洲的世界联合书院（United World Colleges）的 12 所学院之一。该学院每年有来自全球 80 多个国家的 200 多名留学生。所有的学生都以全额奖学金入学。这种优越的国际化经历使学生们超越民族主义，尊重多元化，促进国际间的相互理解和国际社会的改革。

　　该校以加拿大前首相皮尔逊的名字命名，它的全称是 Lester B. Pearson College of the Pacific。

　　皮尔逊在任五年期间，主持建立了加拿大退休金计划（the Canada Pension Plan），国家全民医保体系（National System of Universal Medicare），双语并存和二元文化研究委员会（the Commission on Bilingualism and Biculturalism），并将枫叶旗（Maple Leaf Flag）确定为加拿大国旗。他首倡派遣联合国维和部队解决苏伊士运河争端。由此他于 1957 年获得诺贝尔和平奖。2003 年，在加拿大历史学家、政治学家、经济学家、前任政府官员、以及作家、记者中展开的一项调查显示，皮尔逊被公认为加拿大过去 50 年中最好的首相。他的任期被描述为"加拿大政治历史上激动人心的转折点"。

▶ Detailed Notes to the Text（课文详解）

1. I arrived at Pearson College in Victoria, British Columbia, in late August.

　　1) arrive 后面通常可跟介词 in 或 at，到达的地方如范围较大（如州，国家，大城市），多用 in。例如：

　　When he arrived in Oakland, he took up a room at a small hotel and set to work.

　　他到达奥克兰后，在一个小旅馆找了个房间就开始工作了。

　　They arrived at the station twenty minutes before the train was due.

　　他们在火车出发前 20 分钟到达车站。

　　2) arrive 在和 home, there, here 等副词连用时，不用再加介词。例如：

　　Sofia felt in excellent spirits when she arrived home.

　　索非亚回到家时心情好极了。

　　Arriving there, he made up his mind to go on.

　　到那里后，他下定决心要继续下去。

13

2. I could have gone to the University of Toronto in Ontaria, ...

"could + have done（不定式的完成形式）" 是虚拟语气，表示对过去事情的假设。

1）表示（那时）"本来可以"，"差点就要" 等。例如：

I could have passed the exam, but I was too careless.

我本可以通过考试，但是我太粗心。

I could have lent you the money. Why didn't you ask me?

我本来可以借给你钱的。你怎么不向我开口呢?

2）表示（那时）可能。例如：

I don't see how I could have done otherwise.

我真不知道我还能怎么做。

We could not have heard them because of the noise from the river.

因为河里的噪音我们不可能听得见他们。

3）用来提出婉转的批评（可译为 "其实可以……"）。例如：

You could have been more considerate.

你其实可以表现得更体谅些。

We could have started a little earlier.

我们要是再早一点开始就好了。

3. 1) But I chose this school for its small size and its excellent program in my major field—linguistics.

2) Robert, who is majoring in elementary education, ...

major 在句 1）中为名词，意为 "专业"，这里修饰 field，意为 "主修课程"。例如：

He planned to take chemistry as his major.

他计划主修化学。

History was his major.

历史是他的专业。

它也可表示 "主修……的学生"。例如：

He is a history major.

他是历史专业的学生。

major 在句 2）中为动词，意为 "主修"，常与介词 in 连用。例如：

Betty majors in economics and I major in English.

贝蒂主修经济，而我主修英语。

Christina majored in two subjects at the University of Sydney.

克里斯蒂娜在悉尼大学主修两门课程。

4. I'm taking four courses: ...

take 是一个非常有用的动词，它有很多习惯用法。在此表示的是"选修"。例如：

I plan to take both French and Spanish this term.

本学期我准备选修法语和西班牙语。

There are just two courses you can take.

只有两门课供你选修。

take 还可表示"选择，选购"。例如：

We must have taken a wrong turning.

我们一定是拐错弯了。

I'll take both suits.

我两件都要（买）。

5. ... and the professor often gives us individual instruction during his office hours.

1) individual instruction 意为"个别辅导，单独辅导"，individual 在此为形容词，意为"个人的，个别的"。例如：

Benches are for several people; chairs are individual seats.

长凳是给几个人合坐的，而椅子是单个人坐的。

Each individual leaf on the tree is different.

树上每一片叶子都是不一样的。

Students can apply for individual tutoring.

学生可以申请个别辅导。

2) office hours 指办公时间。例如：

You mustn't take up his time in office hours (办公时间).

你不应占用他的办公时间。

The doctor had office hours four days a week.

大夫每周四次门诊。

6. I've made friends with a Canadian student, ...

make 也是一个常用的英文动词。它有很多固定的搭配用法，make friends（with somebody）就是其中之一，意为"和……成为朋友"。例如：

You'll find us all wanting to make friends with you.

你会发觉我们都想和你交朋友。

She hoped that they would make friends.

她希望他们能成为朋友。

7. ... I have a scholarship...

I work as a language lab assistant...

scholarship 在此意为"奖学金"。work as a language lab assistant 意为"在语言实验室里作助教"。助教奖学金（assistantship）在美国、加拿大的大学里也是一种奖学金形式。

8. My plan for the future is..., and then to devote my life to research in linguistics.

devote 意为"把……献给……，把……用在……"。例如：

Devote the next several minutes to helping the students memorize the dialogue.

下面几分钟都用来帮助学生熟记对话。

Key to Exercises（参考答案）

1. 1) In late August.

   2) Pearson College is a small school.

   3) Pearson College.

   4) The professor often gives them individual instruction.

   5) He gives free lessons to children of poor families in a city nearby.

   6) He has a scholarship.

   7) He works as a language lab assistant to help pay other bills.

   8) His plan for the future is to teach English for a few years in a university and then to devote his life to research in linguistics.

   9) How was his vacation? How many students is he teaching now? Which books is he using this year?

   10) He ends his letter by asking questions.

2. 1) arrived   2) choose   3) enjoy   4) pay   5) majored

   6) chosen   7) paid   8) playing   9) choose   10) enjoy

3. 1) C   2) A   3) D   4) C   5) C

   6) B   7) B   8) B   9) B   10) B

   11) D   12) A   13) D   14) B   15) A

   16) B   17) D   18) A   19) A   20) B

21) C	22) A	23) D	24) C	25) A
26) D	27) A	28) C	29) C	30) B

4. A. 1) Whose exercise book is that?

2) Which building is the post office in?

3) Since when have you been working together?

4) What is your brother like?

5) Which one is better, the first one or the second one?

B. 1) Be diligent in your English study.

2) Get me a Chinese-English dictionary please, Mary.

3) Don't forget to bring your homework here tomorrow.

4) Let's take the matter up with the man in charge.

5) Go and ask him to be true to his own promise.

C. 1) What a lovely day it is today!

2) How foolish he was to do that!

3) How nice it would be if she could come with us!

4) How proud we are of our college!

5) What a charming lady she is!

5. A. 1) They arrived at the station twenty minutes before the train was due.

2) Sofia felt in excellent spirits when she arrived home.

3) Indications are that the accident could have been prevented.

4) I don't see how I could have done otherwise.

5) He is a history major.

6) Betty majors in economics and I major in English.

7) There are just two courses you can take.

8) You'll find us all wanting to make friends with you.

9) He has devoted his whole life to benefiting mankind.

10) The doctor had office hours four days a week.

B. 1) 皮尔逊学院规模不大，与安大略的多伦多大学有很大的不同，多伦多大学又大又有名气。

2) 我和一位加拿大大学生交了朋友，他叫罗伯特·威尔逊。

3) 罗伯特主修基础教育。很多大学生都义务为附近城市贫困家庭的孩子上课，他就是其中之一。

4) 像我的近半数同学一样，我靠奖学金来支付一部分上学费用。

5) 我一直记得您上的那些课，那些课使我受益匪浅。

6) 我哥哥的专业是心理学。

7) 他们说做广告值得。

8) 他是一位负责的医生，并得到了病人的信任。

9) 青年节马上就要到了。

10) 你觉得昨天的音乐会怎么样？

6. 1) C   2) B   3) C   4) A   5) A

     6) B   7) D   8) B   9) C   10) A

7.

Dear Sir or Madam,

    I bought an English-Chinese dictionary in your shop last month when I was in Shanghai on business. When I got home, I found dozens of pages of the dictionary were missing. Now I send you the dictionary with this letter and strongly wish that you could send me a new one soon.

Yours faithfully,
Wang Min

Reading:

1. 1) C   2) A   3) D   4) C   5) A

2. 1) F   2) F   3) T   4) F   5) T

Listening:

1. W: Shall we take an umbrella with us?

    M: No need to. It is not likely to rain.

    Q: What is the weather like?

2. W: Perhaps the weather will change this evening.

    M: Perhaps it will, perhaps it won't.

    Q: Do you think the man agrees with the woman?

3. M: I can't understand why my friend isn't here yet. Do you think we should try to call her or go look for her?

W: She probably just got tied up in traffic. Let's give her a few more minutes.

Q: What are these people going to do?

4. M: Which dress do you plan to wear?

W: I like the black one, and it fits me better, but it's probably too modern. I suppose I'll wear the red one.

Q: Why didn't the woman wear the black dress?

5. M: The train's leaving in no time. Jack's late again.

W: He might get here in time, but I can't be sure.

Q: What is Jack like?

Key:

1. C   2. C   3. C   4. B   5. C

Dictation:

Our classroom is on the third floor of Sir Shaw Run Run Building. It is a large room about 20 feet long and 10 feet wide. The walls are light green and the ceiling is white. On the front of the wall, there is a large blackboard with chalk and erasers on the ledge. On its left, there is a brown door. On its right, there are two large windows, under which there are two radiators for heating in the wintertime. There are about 40 light-colored chairs in the room for the students, and the teacher's desk is in the front of the room. On the whole, it is a pleasant and comfortable room, in which we study every day. We like this room.

Chinese Translation（课文参考译文）

写给老师的一封信

（齐亚·阿里来自巴基斯坦。内·汤普森先生是他在巴基斯坦时的英语老师。现在，齐亚正在加拿大的一所学院学习。）

梅里达街 1842 号

不列颠哥伦比亚省，维多利亚

加拿大 V8N 5C9

1999 年 10 月 3 日

亲爱的内·汤普森先生：

　　我于8月下旬到达不列颠哥伦比亚省维多利亚的皮尔逊学院。皮尔逊学院规模不大，和安大略的多伦多大学有很大的不同，多伦多大学又大又有名气。我本来可以去多伦多大学，但是我还是选择了皮尔逊学院，因为它的规模不大，但在我主修的专业，语言学方面开设的课程很优秀。

　　几周以前，我开始上课了，我非常喜欢这些课。我目前修4门课：英语、应用语言学、数学和心理学。上语言学课的学生并不是太多。教授经常在办公时间给我们单独辅导。他是一个善良的老人而且学识渊博。尽管我忙于学习，但我仍然找时间参加足球队的活动。

　　我和一位加拿大同学交了朋友，他叫罗伯特·威尔逊。我们一起在图书馆学习，一起在校园里散步。罗伯特主修基础教育。很多大学生都义务为附近城市贫困家庭的孩子上课，他就是其中之一。

　　像我的近半数同学一样，我靠奖学金来支付一部分上学费用。我还在语言实验室作助教，以支付其他费用。我计划在大学里教几年英语，然后一生致力于语言学的研究。

　　您的假期过得怎样？现在您教多少学生？今年您使用的教材是什么？我一直记着您上的那些课，那些课使我受益匪浅。

您真诚的，

齐亚·阿里

UNIT 3 *Kites*

Background Knowledge（背景知识）

关于风筝的起源，大体有三种传说。一是斗笠、树叶说；二是帆船、帐篷说；三是飞鸟说。但风筝起源于中国，则是目前世界公认的。

斗笠、树叶说

斗笠是一种古老的防雨防暑的器具，当人类由渔猎转为耕作时就开始使用，在热带、亚热带更是必不可少。据说有一农夫正在耕作时，忽然狂风大作，卷起了他的斗笠，农夫赶紧去追，一下抓住系绳。恰巧这系绳很长，农夫抓着绳子的一头，系在绳子另一头的斗笠还在空中继续飞行。农夫觉得非常有趣，以后便经常给村民放斗笠，后来演变成放风筝。

树叶说源于中国南方一带。据说古时候人们对风卷树叶满天飞的现象十分崇拜，便用麻丝等拴住树叶放着玩，逐渐演变成放风筝活动。中国台湾的高山族、海南岛的黎族人，以前就是用面包树的叶子来做风筝的。

帆船、帐篷说

传说禹时已有了帆船。帆可以借助风力，人们仿照帆的原理，扎起风筝放飞。还有人说，风筝起源于北方的帐篷，最早的风筝是人们模仿帐篷被大风刮起在空中飘扬的现象制造出来的，之后演变成了一种娱乐活动。

飞鸟说

从目前的历史记载和发现的古代风筝看，其结构、形状、扎绘技术等，一个突出的特征就是以鸟的形状为主。因而有人得出结论：最初的风筝，是受飞鸟的启发，模仿飞鸟制造出来的。人们崇尚飞鸟、热爱飞鸟、模拟飞鸟而制作风筝，是人们对美好生活的追求。

中国是风筝的发源地，而中国最早的风筝是由古代的思想家墨翟制造的。据《韩非子·外储说》载：

墨翟居鲁山（今山东青州一带），"斫木为鹞，三年而成，飞一日而败。"是说墨子研究了三年，终于用木头制成了一只木鸟，但只飞了一天就坏了。墨子制造的这只"木鹞"就是中国最早的风筝。

> ## ▶ Detailed Notes to the Text （课文详解）

1. 1) They are made in all shapes, colors, and sizes.

2) Some are shaped like fish, ...

shape 在句 1） 中为名词，意为 "形状，模样" （多作可数名词）。例如：

The shape of Italy resembles a boot when you look at it on a map.

地图上的意大利形状像一只靴子。

Hasn't that cloud a strange shape?

那片云的形状不是很奇异吗？

它也可表示 "状况" （不可数）。例如：

That company is in good shape financially.

那个公司财政状况很好。

Henry is in good shape.

亨利身体很好。

shape 在句 2） 中为动词，意为 "使成为某种形状" （多用过去分词作表语或定语）。例如：

The necklace is shaped like a bell.

那项链被做成了一个铃的形状。

A safety-pin is so shaped that it cannot easily prick you.

一种安全别针做成了不易扎人的形状。

a cloud shaped like a camel

一朵形状像骆驼的云

a heart-shaped cake

一块心形蛋糕

它也可表示 "使成形，使发展成某种样子"。例如：

A good teacher helps shape a child's character.

一位好老师会帮助塑造孩子的性格。

This event shaped his whole life.

这一事件影响了他的一生。

2. Then all that is needed is a cloth tail for balance...

all 和一个定语从句连用在此表示 "所……只是，所……一切"。它的用法包括

1） 作主语。例如：

All's well that ends well.

结果好就一切都好。

All that glitters is not gold.

闪光的不都是金子。

All you have to do is to listen.

你唯一该做的就是听。

2) 作宾语或介词宾语。例如：

I have said all I intend to say.

我想说的都说了。

You've seen all there is to see.

能看到的你都看到了。

3) 作表语。例如：

Is that all you want to say?

你想说的都说完了吗？

That's all there is to be said.

能说的都说完了。

3. Most kite fans fly their kites just for fun, but serious kite fliers enter contests and tournaments.

for fun 表示"为高兴，为好玩"。例如：

He's learning French for fun.

他学法语是为了好玩。

I did it only for fun.

我只是为了高兴才那样做的。

enter 最常用的意思为"进入，进来"，但在此处它表示"参加，到……里面工作"。例如：

I refused to enter the discussion.

我拒绝参加讨论。

If you plan to enter the diplomatic corps, study history and foreign languages.

你如果想进入外交使团，就学习历史和外语吧。

4. These events are conducted under the rules of the International Kite fliers' Association.

conduct 在此表示"进行"。例如：

He should learn how to conduct a meeting.

他应学会如何主持会议。

Businessmen, authors and actors all may hire agents to conduct their affairs.

商人、作者和演员都可以雇用代理来打理他们的事务。

conduct an experiment

做一个实验

conduct a survey

进行一次调查

rules 在此表示"规则，规定"（可数）。例如：

You must obey the rules of the game.

你必须遵守游戏规则。

The members of the club make the rules.

由俱乐部会员制定规则。

5. Kites are used for practical purposes, too.

practical 表示"实际的，现实的"。例如：

I don't think that it would be of much practical value to either of us.

我认为这对我们两个都没有什么实际价值。

It sounds like a good idea, but there are some practical difficulties.

听起来是个好主意，但还有些实际困难。

practical 还可表示"切实可行的，实用的"。例如：

He gave sound and practical advice.

他给出了既合理又切实可行的建议。

Your invention is clever, but not very practical.

你的发明很巧妙，但不太实用。

6. Some of the kites used in this work carry scientific instruments, ...

carry 在此意为"携带"。例如：

I carried the box up the stairs.

我把箱子搬上了楼。

I never carry much money about me.

我从不在身上带很多钱。

These pipes carry water to the town.

这些管道把水输送进城。

carry 还可和自身代词连用，表示"举止，姿态，体态"。例如：

She carries herself very well.

她体态优美。

He carries himself like a soldier.

他的举止像个士兵。

成语用法 carry away 表示"使激动得失去控制，使倾倒"。例如：

The audience was carried away by the speaker's eloquence.

演讲者的口才打动了听众。

He let his anger carry him away.

他怒不可遏。

7. To launch a kite, it's usually necessary to run into the wind for a few feet.

run into 在此意为"迎着风"。一般情况下，它表示"和……相撞"。例如：

The car skidded and ran into a lamp-post.

汽车打滑撞到了灯柱上。

Joe lost control of his bike and ran into a tree.

乔伊自行车失控撞到了树上。

它还表示"无意间碰到"。例如：

Lester did not expect to run into many of his friends.

莱斯特没想到会碰上那么多朋友。

8. As the kite begins to rise, let out more line and give some short tugs.

tug 为名词，意为"拉，扯，拽"。例如：

Give the drawer a tug and it will open.

拉一下抽屉，它就会开。

Give it a good tug.

使劲拉（拽）。

▶ Supplementary Grammar （语法补充材料）

冠词的一些习惯用法

1）定冠词。例如：

in the morning/afternoon/evening	早上（下午，晚上）
tell the truth	说真话
go to the theatre	看戏
go to the doctor	看病
on the horizon	在地平线上
a man in the street	普通人
beg the question	用未证实的假定为论据（以回避正题）

break the ice	打破沉默
bite the bullet	硬着头皮去做难做的事
burn the midnight oil	开夜车
put the blame on...	归咎于
pass the buck to...	推卸责任给（某人）
drink someone under the table	灌醉某人
put the cart before the horse	本末倒置
strike while the iron is hot	趁热打铁

2) 不定冠词。例如：

make a fuss	大惊小怪
with a will	起劲地
be a credit to (one's family, school, etc.)	为（家庭，学校等）争光
wait for an eternity	无休止地等待
make a racket	大声喧闹
beat a retreat	撤退
take a bow	谢幕
have a liking for	喜欢
make a scene	当众大闹
all of a sudden	突然
as a rule	通常
as a matter of fact	事实上

3) 零冠词。例如：

cast anchor	抛锚	catch fire	着火
change course	改变方向	delay sentence	推迟判决
give way	让路	keep home	管理家务
leave school	离校，毕业	lose heart	丧失信心
make way	前进	send word	捎信
set sail	启航	take root	扎根
take shape	成形	talk sense	说有意义的话
at home	在家	by chance	偶然
by day	白天	learn by heart	记住
for show	作秀（给别人看）	in time	及时
in charge	主管	in haste	匆忙地

on foot	步行	on hand	在手头
out of date	过时	out of place	不适当的（时机）
out of mind	忘却	under cover	隐蔽地
without question	毫无疑问	on account of	因为
by courtesy of	承蒙……允许	in front of	在前面
in spite of	尽管	catch sight of	看到
find fault with	挑剔	get wind of	听到风声
make use of	利用	take hold of	抓住
keep pace with...	与……齐步前进		

4）其他习语

A. prison, school, university, college, church, hospital 等名词前为零冠词时，不表示具体的地点或机构，而表示在该地方进行的活动。例如：

I went to school when I was seven years old.

我七岁开始上学。（去上学）

Mr. Smith went to the school to see his daughter's teacher.

史密斯先生到学校去见他女儿的老师。（到学校去）

Mrs. Kelly goes to church every Sunday.

凯丽太太每星期天去教堂。（去做礼拜）

The workmen went to the church to repair the roof.

工人们到教堂去修屋顶。（指教堂的建筑物）

Ken is in prison for robbery.

凯恩由于抢劫而坐牢。（凯恩是囚犯）

Ken went to the prison to visit his brother.

凯恩去监狱看他弟弟。（凯恩是探监人）

B. 地名

洲名前用零冠词。例如：

Africa	非洲	Asia	亚洲
Europe	欧洲	South America	南美洲

国名前一般用零冠词。例如：

France	法国	China	中国
Japan	日本	Nigeria	尼日利亚

但国名为复合名词或复数时，要用定冠词。例如：

the United States of America	美国
the United Kingdom	英国

the United Arab Emirates   阿拉伯联合酋长国

the Philippines   菲律宾

the Netherlands   荷兰

城镇名前一般用零冠词。例如：

Cairo	开罗	Beijing	北京
New York	纽约	Madrid	马德里

但也有例外。如：The Hague   海牙

地区名一般加定冠词。例如：

the Middle East   中东

the Far East   远东

the north of England   英格兰北部

但用方向性形容词时，地区名前面不加定冠词。例如：

northern England   英格兰北部

southern Spain   西班牙南部

western Canada   加拿大西部

山脉名一般为复数，前面加定冠词。例如：

the Rocky Mountains   落基山脉

the Alps   阿尔卑斯山脉

the Andes   安第斯山脉

海洋、河流、运河名前面一般加定冠词。例如：

the Pacific (Ocean)   太平洋

the Atlantic (Ocean)   大西洋

the Indian Ocean   印度洋

the Mediterranean (Sea)   地中海

the (English) Channel   英吉利海峡

the Nile   尼罗河

注意，地图上标注时一般都不加定冠词。

街道、广场名前一般加零冠词。例如：

Broadway   百老汇大街

Fifth Avenue   第五街

Piccadilly Circus   皮卡迪利广场

Tian An Men Square   天安门广场

用人名、地名命名的地方前一般加零冠词。例如：

Kennedy Airport   肯尼迪机场

Cambridge University   剑桥大学

Hyde Park	海德公园
Westminster	威斯敏斯特大教堂
Barclay's Bank	巴克利银行（英国）

Key to Exercises（参考答案）

1. 1) In Korea Peninsula, Japan and China.

2) On the first few days of the year.

3) A simple kite can be made with two crossed pieces of light wood glued to a sheet of paper or plastic.

4) Some are shaped like fish, dragons or birds.

5) A cloth tail.

6) Most kite fans fly their kites just for fun.

7) The US Weather Bureau uses kites to gather information about winds and weather. Some of the kites used in this work carry scientific instruments and fly higher than 20,000 feet.

8) To launch a kite, it's usually necessary to run into the wind for a few feet.

9) As the kite begins to rise, let out more line and give it some short tugs.

10) Because it is very dangerous.

2. 1) rises 2) entered 3) has been conducted 4) need 5) was held
6) gather 7) are flown 8) is shaped 9) use 10) glued

3. A. 1) C 2) D 3) A 4) C 5) B
6) B 7) B 8) D 9) A 10) A
11) D 12) B 13) B 14) A 15) C
16) B 17) D 18) D 19) B 20) C□

B. 1) B 2) B 3) A 4) B 5) A
6) A 7) A 8) B 9) C 10) C
11) D 12) B 13) C 14) A 15) C

4. A. 1) Kites are flown in many parts of the world.

2) Pink is the most popular colour this year.

3) The Spring Festival is an important part of Chinese culture.

4) The machine is made in the USA.

5) They study English for fun.

6) The computer is one of the most practical office equipments.

7) Rice and dumplings are the favourite food of Chinese people.

8) Our purpose to learn English well is to do our work better.

9) There is a hospital near our school.

10) Christmas is the most important festival in the West.

B. 1) 几千年以来，生活在世界许多地方的不同年龄的人都制作并放风筝。

2) 在中国，每年都有一天作为风筝节来庆祝。

3) 风筝被制作成各种形状，颜色和大小也各不相同。一些风筝的形状像鱼、龙或者鸟。

4) 这些活动按国际风筝协会的规则进行。

5) 一个简单的风筝是将两条交叉成十字型的轻木条和一张纸或塑料粘在一起制作而成的。

6) 大多数风筝迷放风筝只是为了娱乐，但是认真的放风筝的人会参加比赛。

7) 风筝也有实际功用。

8) 美国气象局利用风筝收集关于风和气象的信息。

9) 放风筝通常需要迎风跑几步。

10) 不要在靠近树林和电线的地方放风筝。

5. 1) A　　　　2) D　　　　3) C　　　　4) B　　　　5) A
   6) D　　　　7) A　　　　8) D　　　　9) C　　　　10) B

Reading:

1. 1) D　　　　2) D　　　　3) D　　　　4) C　　　　5) D

2. 1) T　　　　2) F　　　　3) F　　　　4) T　　　　5) F

Listening:

1. M: Excuse me. Is this seat taken?

   W: I don't think so. The man who was seating here went out five minutes ago.

   Q: Where did the conversation most possibly take place?

2. W: Do you have any reason to believe your passport was stolen?

   M: Yes, I left it in my car an hour ago, and it's not there now.

   Q: What does the man believe?

3. M: Why are you interested in working in our company?

   W: Well, I believe I'll have a better future if I can work with your company.

   Q: What can we learn from the conversation?

4. M: I'm not sure whether to buy a new computer or a second-hand one.

   W: In the long run, to buy a new one saves money.

   Q: What does the woman advise the man to do?

5. M: Can I rent a room for 2 weeks? I am not sure whether I will stay for a whole month.

   W: Yes, it is $150 for a week, but only $400 for a month.

   Q: How much should the man pay if he rents the room for 2 weeks?

Key:

| 1. A | 2. D | 3. A | 4. D | 5. C |

Dictation:

   We interrupt this programme to bring you a piece of special news. The Weather Station reports that a heavy thunderstorm is coming within about two hours. We'll be experiencing high winds and driving rains with a lot of thunder and lightning. Travellers are warned to stay off roads during the storm. Further information about the weather will follow immediately after the programme.

Chinese Translation（课文参考译文）

风筝

   几千年以来、生活在世界许多地方的不同年龄的人们都制作风筝并放风筝。在朝鲜半岛，人们在一年的头几天放风筝，把它作为一种庆祝活动。在日本，放风筝是每年五月举行的男孩节的一个重要组成部分。在中国，每年都有一天作为风筝节来庆祝。在这些特别的风筝庆典上，成千上万的风筝被放飞。它们被制作成各种形状，颜色和大小也各不相同。一些风筝的形状像鱼、龙或鸟。所有的风筝都非常鲜艳多彩。

   一个简单的风筝是将两条交叉成十字型的轻木条和一张纸或塑料粘在一起制作而成的。其次，还需要一个用布做的尾巴来保持平衡，还有一团线绳，当然还需要适宜的风。

   大多数风筝迷放风筝只是为了娱乐，但是认真的放风筝的人会参加比赛。这些活动按照国际风筝放飞者协会的规则进行。风筝也有实际功用。美国气象局利用风筝收集关于风和气象的信息。一些用于此用途的风筝可携带科学仪器飞到 20,000 英尺以上的高空。

平面风筝是最简单、最常见的风筝。箱型风筝也很流行。还有一种受欢迎的风筝看起来像飞鸟。

放风筝通常需要迎风跑几步。随着风筝开始上升，多放一些线出去，再轻轻地拉一拉风筝。

不要在靠近树林和电线的地方放风筝。另外，你不能在有飞机低空飞行的地方放风筝。

UNIT 4   *Late One Evening*

Background Knowledge（背景知识）

在读到本单元课文《一天深夜》的巧妙结尾时，我们会禁不住发出会心的微笑。

很多优秀的作者善于利用幽默来达到一定的艺术效果。本课中，我们将着重介绍美国小说家欧·亨利（O. Henry, 1862—1910）。欧·亨利笔调幽默，构思精巧，风格独特，并善于用双关语。他的小说的结尾往往既出人意料又合乎情理，这就是闻名于世的"欧·亨利式结尾"。

中国读者对欧·亨利的不少名篇并不陌生，如"最后一片叶子"(The Last Leaf)、"爱的牺牲"(A Service of Love)、"咖啡馆里的世界公民"(A Cosmopolite in a Cafe)、"麦琪的礼物"(The Gift of Magi)、"警察与赞美诗"(The Cop and the Anthem)等。

下面，我们就以"警察与赞美诗"为例，来欣赏著名的"欧·亨利式结尾"。故事的主人公叫索比（Soapy），是纽约市的一个无家可归者。他计划到布莱克韦尔岛——一所有名的监狱去度过严冬。在那里，"有饭吃，有床睡，还有志趣相投的伙伴，而且不受'北风'和警察的侵扰。"

为达到这个目的，他尝试了许多途径。例如他打算先在一家灯火辉煌的咖啡馆里美食一顿，然后让侍者把他交给警察，送进监狱。可是穿着破旧的他刚踏进门，就被侍者推了出去。

随后他捡起鹅卵石砸碎了路边装潢精美的大玻璃橱窗，等着被警察抓走。但闻声赶来的警察却不相信索比是肇事者，因为他没有仓皇逃走。

索比又来到一家不太招眼的餐厅，大吃一顿后对侍者说，"现在，赶快去叫警察，别让大爷久等。"然而侍者根本没去找警察，而是把他"干净利落地推倒在又冷又硬的人行道上，左耳贴着地。"

索比继续在街上游荡，看到一位"衣着简朴却又讨人喜欢的年轻女人站在橱窗前"，两码以外站着一个魁梧的警察。他公然调戏那个女人，没想到她是个风尘女子，竟然缠着他不放。到了拐弯处，索比撒腿就跑，甩掉了这位女伴。

他在大街上扯开破锣似的嗓子像醉汉一样胡闹，故意"扰乱治安"，但警察却以为他是个"耶鲁小子"在庆祝校际赛的胜利，说"上级有指示，让他们闹去吧。"

他到雪茄烟店，随便拿了一位顾客的绸伞就走。顾客追了出来，索比让他叫警察，但这位顾客却承认那把伞是他捡到的，他以为索比才是这把绸伞的主人。

最后，索比来到了一座古老的教堂边，听着风琴师练习星期天的赞美诗，他的灵魂猛然间出现了奇妙的变化，"在他的内心深处引起了一场革命。"他下决心要改邪归正，第二天就去找一份正当的工作。

然而，就在此时，一名警察出现在他面前并逮捕了他。第二天早晨法官宣判："布莱克韦尔岛，三个月。"

这就是"欧·亨利式结尾"，它出人意料又合乎情理，让人忍俊不禁，又发人深省。

Detailed Notes to the Text（课文详解）

1. ... a friend and I were making our way merrily home...

make our way merrily home 在此表示"很高兴地往家走"。make one's way 是习惯用法，表示"前往，前进"。例如：

The two women made their way into the woods.

那两个女人走进了树林。

He made his way by scholarships through Oxford.

他靠奖学金上完了牛津大学。

2. We had been to a musical, ...

musical 在此为名词，意为"音乐喜剧"，"音乐片"。例如：

John had three musicals playing in London at one time.

约翰曾经在伦敦同时上演过三个音乐剧。

musical 也可作形容词，意为"音乐的，爱好音乐的，悦耳的"。例如：

Helen can play nearly every musical instrument.

海伦几乎会演奏所有的乐器。

I guess I don't have any musical talent.

我想我是个没有音乐天分的人。

3. "That show made him a star overnight," ...

make 在此跟由名词构成的复合结构，意为"使得，成为"。例如：

All work and no play makes Jack a dull boy.

只工作不玩耍，聪明孩子也变傻。

He finally made her his wife.

他最终娶了她。

此结构可用于被动语态。例如：

Newton was made President of the Royal Society.

牛顿成了皇家学会的主席。

He has been made a scapegoat of the ruling circles and compelled to resign.

他成了统治集团的替罪羊而被迫辞职。

4. "I thought him quite good," I said, "but not worth thousands of love letters daily. ..."

worth 在此表示"值得"，后面可跟名词或代词。例如：

Is it worth all the trouble?

这么麻烦的事值得去做吗？

The exhibition is well worth a visit.

那个展览值得参观。

She sometimes asked herself the question whether it was worth the effort.

有时她会问自己付出这些努力是不是值得。

worth 也可跟动名词。例如：

It's worth trying, isn't it?

值得一试，不是吗？

Chengdu is a city worth visiting.

成都是个值得参观的城市。

What is worth doing is worth doing well.

值得做的事就值得把它做好。

5. As a matter of fact, one of his songs gave me a pain.

pain 在此是口语用法，表示"令人厌烦的人或事物"。例如：

She's been complaining again—she's a real pain!

她又发牢骚了，真烦人！

We've missed the last bus—what a pain!

我们没赶上末班公共汽车——真倒霉！

pain 的复数还可表示"努力，功夫，费事"。例如：

No pains, no gains.

没有耕耘就没有收获。

All he got for his pains was ingratitude and suspicion.

他付出那么多，得到的却只是忘恩负义和怀疑。

6. I burst into a parody of the song.

burst into 在此表示 "突然（进入某种状态或发生某种情况）"。例如：

When he took the floor, the gathering burst into thunderous applause.

当他演说时，听众爆发出雷鸣般的掌声。

As soon as she saw me, she burst into tears.

她一见到我就大哭起来。

The orchards seemed to have burst into blossom overnight.

果园好像一夜之间就开出了满园的花朵。

7. My friend had given me an astonished look.

astonish 表示 "使惊异，使大为吃惊"，多用过去分词作表语。例如：

He was probably astonished to see his father.

见到他的父亲，他可能很惊讶。

You look astonished at the news.

听到那个消息你看上去很吃惊。

I'm astonished that he didn't come.

他没来我感到很惊讶。

astonished 有时也可用作定语或状语。例如：

Richard gave her an astonished look.

理查德很惊讶地看了她一眼。

Shelley, astonished, urged her to explain.

雪莉感到很惊奇，迫切地要她做出解释。

8. You'll give everybody a fright and wake people up for miles around.

fright 在此表示 "惊吓（可数）"。例如：

You gave me a fright by knocking so loudly on the door.

你敲门这么响，吓了我一跳。

I got the fright of my life when the machine burst into flames.

让我一生中最害怕的是那次机器突然起火。

fright 也可表示 "惊吓，害怕（不可数）"。例如：

Margaret was staring at me with pity, with something like fright.

玛格利特用怜悯的眼光盯着我，似乎受到了惊吓。

I nearly died of fright at the sight of the escaped lion.

看到那只逃出来的狮子我吓得要死。

Fright gave the old lady heart failure.

由于惊吓老妇人心脏病发作了。

9. ... I said, intoxicated more with the sound of my own voice than with the few drinks we had had.

intoxicate 表示 "使沉醉，使陶醉"。例如：

Tom was intoxicated knowing that at last he had gained his degree and would be financially independent.

当得知自己终于获得了学位并将在经济上独立时，汤姆欣喜若狂。

The joy of victory so intoxicated him that he jumped and sang and behaved like a crazy man.

他陶醉在胜利的喜悦中，发疯一般地唱啊，跳啊。

intoxicated 常用作过去分词作表语，表示 "喝醉"，"陶醉"。例如：

How could she become intoxicated after only one glass of wine?

她怎么会只喝了一杯酒就醉了呢？

An intoxicated man loses control of himself.

喝醉酒的人通常失去自控能力。

10. And I went on singing him the latest tunes at the top of my voice.

at the top of one's voice 表示 "高声地"。例如：

He shouted suddenly at the top of his voice.

他突然高声地喊了起来。

Everyone's yelling at the top of his voice.

每个人都扯着嗓门大喊。

11. ... and before you could say "Jack Robinson", a policeman was standing in front of me, his notebook open, a determined look on his face.

his notebook open, a determined look on his face 是独立结构，常用作状语，在它之前也可用介词 with，这时意义并无变化，只是较为口语化而已。例如：

The teacher entered the classroom, with a book in his hand.

老师拿着书进了教室。

12. ... "you have a remarkable voice, if I may say so..."

if I may say so 是一种客气的表达方式，类似的有 if you like, if you please。例如：

If you like, we can drop in on Saturday evening.

如果方便的话，我们将在周六晚上来你家。

If you please, sir, can you direct me to the town Square?

先生，如果不打扰您的话，您能告诉我去市区广场怎么走吗？

13. Then my wife or I would drop you a line...

drop a line 意为"写信给某人"。例如：

I must drop a line to my uncle to thank him for having us.

我要给叔叔写信感谢他接待了我们。

Drop us a line to let us know how you are getting on.

写封信告诉我们你近况如何。

► Supplementary Grammar（语法补充材料）

代词（二）

6. 指示代词

6.1 指示代词的形式

指示代词专门用来指出或标示人或物，它们是：this（这个），that（那个），these（这些），those（那些）。

6.2 指示代词在句子中的功用为：

1）作定语。例如：

This motor-car is for hire.

这辆车供租用。

If those clouds drift away, we'll have a fine afternoon.

要是那些云散开了，下午天气就好了。

2）作主语。例如：

Anyway, this can wait.

至少，这事可以暂时搁置。

Are these what you want?

这些就是你想要的吗？

3）作宾语。例如：

We can in no way allow this to continue.

我们决不允许这事再继续下去了。

I shall take those.

我将买下那些东西。

4）作表语。例如：

This is not my bag. Mine is <u>that</u> over there.

这不是我的包。我的是那边那个。

5）this（these）指空间或时间上较近的事物；that（those）指空间或时间上较远的事物。例如：

You can't swim at this time of the year.

你不能在这个时节游泳。

That happened twenty years ago.

那事发生在二十年前。

6）that（those）常用来指前面已经讲到过的事物；this（these）常用来指后面将要讲到的事物。例如：

So <u>that</u> is how the matter stands at present.

这就是此事的现状。

I want to know <u>this</u>: Has this Mrs. Jones been here the whole morning?

我就想知道：这位琼斯夫人是否一上午都在这里？

7）作状语，表示程度。例如：

Is it this hot every day?

每天都有这么热吗？

I'm not that stupid!

我还没有那么笨！

7. 疑问代词

疑问代词有 who（谁，主格），whom（谁，宾格），whose（谁的，属格），what（什么），which（哪个，哪些，主、宾格形式相同）等。其中 who, whom 只能指人，what, whose 和 which 可指人或物。疑问代词引导的疑问句为特殊疑问句。疑问代词一般都位于疑问句的句首，并作为句子的某一成分（如主语，宾语，表语等）。例如：

Who is to take the chair?

谁当主席？

Whom/Who are you talking about?

你们在谈论谁？

Whose fault is it but hers?

除了她，还能是谁的错？

What colour is the chair?

椅子是什么颜色？

Which of you has got a computer at home?

你们谁家里有电脑？

Which university did you go to, Oxford or Cambridge?

你在哪个大学学习？牛津还是剑桥？

8. 关系代词

8.1 关系代词的形式

关系代词用于引导定语从句，主要形式为：

1）用于引导限定性定语从句的有：

格 ＼ 指代	人	物
主格	who, that, as	that (which), as
宾格	who/whom, that, as	that (which), as
属格	whose	whose / of which

2）用于非限制性定语从句

格 ＼ 指代	人	物
主格	who, as	which, as
宾格	who/whom, as	which, as
属格	whose	whose / of which

关系代词一方面在从句内担任一种成分，即从句中的主语，宾语，表语或定语；另一方面又代表主句中的一个名词或代词（称为先行词）。例如：

The man who told me this refused to give me his name.

告诉我这件事的那个人拒绝说出他的姓名。(who 在定语从句中为主语，又指主句中的主语 The man。)

8.2 关系代词的用法

that 引导限定性定语从句。例如：

He that would eat the fruit must climb the tree.

欲尝果实，必须付出劳动。(that 作从句中的主语，也可用 who。)

She is the girl that you saw in school.

她就是你在学校里见到的女孩。(that 作从句中的宾语，在这种情况下，常可省略。)

who/whom, whose, which 具有两种功用：1）引导限定性定语从句 2）引导非限定性定语从句。

who/whom 的先行词通常指人，主格用 who，宾格用 whom。例如：

Do you know the boys who are playing football over there?

你认识正在那边踢球的那些男孩吗？

I wanted to find someone with <u>whom</u> I could discuss books and music.

我想找一个可以和我讨论书籍和音乐的人。

在口语中，whom 常可用 who 替代，也可省略。例如：

Look, there are some people here <u>who</u> I want you to meet.

这儿有几个人，我想让你见见。

非限定性定语从句中，做宾语时都用 whom，且不能省略。例如：

My gardener, <u>who</u> is very pessimistic, says there will be no apples this year.

我家的园丁很悲观，他预计今年园子里不会结苹果了。

That morning there was a search for Sophia, <u>whom</u> no one had seen since dinner.

那天上午大家到处找索菲亚，前一天晚饭后就没有人再见过她。

whose 引导的词语与先行词之间是所有关系。例如：

The woman <u>whose</u> umbrella you took is very angry about it.

你拿走了那位女士的伞，她对此很生气。

Ann, <u>whose</u> children are at school all day, is trying to get a job.

安的孩子们全天都上学，所以她正在想办法找份工作。

whose 也可指代"动物"或"无生命的东西"。例如：

The factory, <u>whose</u> workers are all women, is closed for part of the school holidays.

这个工厂的工人都是妇女，所以遇到学校的部分假日工厂就关闭。

which 在从句中作主语时，限定性定语从句中一般可用 that 替代。例如：

He lives in the house <u>which/that</u> is opposite ours.

他住在我们家对面的房子里。

which 在从句中作宾语时，可以用 that 替代，也可以省略。例如：

This is the house (<u>which/that</u>) I built.

这是我盖的房子。

如 which 作宾语时紧跟在介词之后，不能用 that 代替。例如：

This is a subject about <u>which</u> we might argue for a long while.

这是一个我们会争论很长时间的话题。

有时 which 不是代表一个名词，而是代表前面的整个句子或它的一部分意思。例如：

Jack drove too fast, <u>which</u> was reckless.

杰克开车太快，这样做实在太鲁莽。

9. 连接代词

9.1 连接代词的形式

连接代词的形式与关系代词相似。但关系代词引导的是定语从句，而连接代词引导的是名词性从句（主语从句，宾语从句或表语从句）。比较：

He who laughs last laughs best.

谁笑到最后，谁笑得最好。(who 在此为关系代词，引起定语从句 who laughs last，修饰 He)

Who breaks pays.

损坏者必赔偿。(who breaks 为主语从句，其中 who 为连接代词，相当于 anyone who)

Show me what you bought.

把你买的东西给我看看。(what you bought 为宾语从句，其中 what 为连接代词，相当于 the thing which)

10. 不定代词

不定代词为不确定指某人或某物的代词，它们有 all, each, every, both, either, neither, one, none, little, few, many, much, other (s), another, some, any, no；还有由 some, any, no, every 构成的合成代词：

词首 ＼ 词尾	-one	-body	-thing
some-	someone	somebody	something
any-	anyone	anybody	anything
no-	no one / none	nobody	nothing
every-	everyone	everybody	everything

不定代词多数都能做主语，宾语，表语或定语，但含有 some-, any-, no-, every- 的合成代词不能作定语，而 every 和 no 只能作定语。

1）作主语。例如：

All that glitters is not gold.

发光的东西并不都是金子。

Is everybody here?

大家都到了吗?

2）作宾语。例如：

I am speaking for myself, not others.

我的发言只代表自己，不代表其他人。

I've got everything set.

我一切都准备好了。

3）作表语。例如：

That's all for today. Class is dismissed.

今天就讲这些，现在下课。

He is somebody in his own town, but nobody here.

他在家乡是个头面人物，可在这里就是无名小卒了。

4) 作定语。例如：

Let me have <u>another</u> cup of tea.

给我再来一杯茶。

<u>Every</u> couple is not a pair.

并不是每对夫妻都是美满姻缘。

Key to Exercises (参考答案)

1. 1) Long after most people had gone to bed, the writer and his friend walked home.

2) They had been to a musical.

3) They were talking about the people they had seen and heard in the musical.

4) That show made one of the actors a star overnight. But he had not been popular before.

5) He thought him quite good, but not worth thousands of love letters.

6) He began to sing one of the songs in the musical which gave him a pain.

7) His friend thought that he would give everybody a fright and wake people up for miles around.

8) Soon they heard the sound of a heavy tread and a policeman appeared in front of them.

9) He'd very much like to find someone who could give his daughter singing lessons.

10) Open to discussion.

2. 1) overnight   2) went on   3) drop, a line

4) remarkable   5) deserted   6) at the top of her voice

7) presently   8) for the sake of   9) completely

10) As a matter of fact

3. A. 1) C   2) D   3) B   4) A   5) D

6) C   7) A   8) B   9) D   10) D

11) A   12) C   13) D   14) C   15) A

16) B   17) B   18) B   19) B   20) C

B. 1) B   2) D   3) D   4) C   5) C

6) D   7) C   8) B   9) D   10) D

11) B   12) C   13) A   14) B   15) A

4. A. 1) After we got off the train, we made our way to the hotel.

   2) Thousands of people are studying English in Beijing.

   3) Beijing is a beautiful city; it is worth visiting.

   4) On hearing the sad news, she burst into crying.

   5) The student has read quite a few English books. Besides, he has translated an English poem.

   6) Though they were very tired, they went on working.

   7) She had been singing until we appeared.

   8) When he called me, I had gone to bed.

   9) She said that she had been waiting for you for two hours.

   10) When Tom told me the news, I had already known it.

   B. 1) 一天夜晚，人们大多早已入睡了，街上几乎没有人，我和一位朋友穿过寂静无人的街道，高兴地往家里走。

   2) 我们刚刚看过一场音乐剧，正谈论着我们在剧中看到和听到的人物。

   3) 从前，他一点名气也没有。现在，成千上万的青少年给他送巧克力，给他写情书。

   4) 我说：“我认为他挺好，但也不至于每天收到上千封情书。”

   5) 我马上大声并滑稽地模仿起来。

   6) 我的朋友惊异地看了我一眼。

   7) “没关系，”我说。与其说是多喝了几杯，不如说是被自己的嗓音所陶醉。

   8) 突然，一个警察站在我面前，笔记本已经翻开，脸上一副坚定的神色。

   9) 你的嗓音真棒，如果我可以这么说的话。

   10) 你能告诉我你的姓名和地址吗？

5. 1) D   2) C   3) D   4) B   5) B
   6) D   7) C   8) B   9) A   10) B

6.

Football Match

China vs. Japan

Place: Capital Stadium

Time: 7:30 p.m., May 10th

Please contact the students union for tickets, 100 yuan each. Only 60 tickets are available. The goers are expected to gather in front of the school gate at 6 p.m. that day. A school bus will take us to the Capital Stadium.

Reading:

1. 1) C   2) A   3) D   4) D   5) C

2. 1) F   2) T   3) T   4) T   5) T

Listening:

1. M: Let's go for a nice long walk into the country this morning.

   W: I'd like to, but I think I'm catching a cold.

   Q: What will the woman probably do?

2. M: I thought you would be in class till 3 o'clock today.

   W: I usually am. But Professor Smith let us out earlier.

   Q: What can we learn from the conversation?

3. M: I wish we'd taken an umbrella.

   W: that's my fault. I thought it wouldn't rain today.

   Q: What happened to the two speakers?

4. W: I'm so tired. I don't think I can finish this report.

   M: Go home now. Leave that for me.

   Q: What does the man offer to do?

5. M: I guess you like the novel very much.

   W: Yes, it's very interesting. I couldn't help reading it time and again.

   Q: How did the woman feel about the novel?

Key:

1. B   2. C   3. C   4. D   5. B

Dictation:

The Red Cross is an international organization, which cares for people who are in need of help. A man in a Paris hospital who needs blood, a woman in Mexico who was injured in an earthquake, and a family in India that lost their home in a storm may all be aided by the Red Cross. The idea of forming an organization to help the sick and wounded during a war started with Jean Henri Dunant (J. H. 杜南，瑞士慈善家).

The American Red Cross was set up by Clara Barton in 1881. Today the Red Cross in the United States provides a number of services for the public, such as helping people in need, teaching first aid and providing blood.

Chinese Translation（课文参考译文）

一天深夜

一天夜晚，人们大多早已入睡了，街上几乎没有人，我和一位朋友穿过寂静无人的街道，高兴地往家里走。我们刚刚看过一场音乐剧，正谈论着我们在剧中看到和听到的人物。

"那场演出使他一夜成名。"我的朋友谈论着剧中的一位演员。"从前，他一点名气也没有。现在，成千上万的青少年给他送巧克力，给他写情书。"

我说："我认为他挺好，但也不至于每天收到上千封情书。其实，他的一首歌让我很不舒服。"

"哪首歌？"我的朋友问道，"给我唱一唱。"

我马上大声并滑稽地模仿起来。

"看在老天的份上，请别唱了。"我的朋友惊异地看了我一眼。"你会吓着别人，还会把周围数英里的人吵醒。他们还会认为我们俩都是酒鬼。等会儿警察也会来抓咱们。"

"没关系。"我说。与其说是多喝了几杯，不如说是被自己的嗓音所陶醉。"没事，这有什么关系？"我继续用最高的嗓音给他唱最流行的曲调。

一会儿，我们身后传来沉重的脚步声，突然，一个警察站在我面前，笔记本已经翻开，脸上一副坚定的神色。

"对不起，先生，"他说，"你的嗓音真棒，如果我可以这么说的话。谁教你唱歌的？我正想找一位能教我女儿唱歌的人。你能告诉我你的姓名和地址吗？我或我的妻子好与你联系并商量此事。"

Fire! Fire!

Background Knowledge（背景知识）

上一课我们介绍了欧·亨利式的幽默，这里再通过一篇博客文章了解一下"英式幽默"。

遭遇"英式幽默"

很多西方人自我介绍的时候喜欢说"我很有幽默感"，他们大都觉得那是一个优点。但如果你遇到一个很有幽默感的英国人，他的"幽默"是逗乐的还是令你"烦恼"的就不得而知了。

我先生是个英国人。他从来就不肯直接地把话说出来，好像不用幽默就说不了话了。这种幽默已经不仅仅是博人博己一笑的问题，而是一种无休止的智力游戏。由于语言、习惯和背景的原因，英国人之间很容易理解对方的幽默。他们有自己的一套双语用词模式，即用别的词语来指他们都知道的事物。所以俚语的词汇量到如今越来越大。

有一次我们在别的国家度假，在餐馆用餐后，侍者问我们用什么方式付账，他说"塑料"（plastic），侍者听得莫名其妙，当然没想到他指的是信用卡。

不过说实话，他的幽默除了制造了很多困扰，还是有令我开心的时候。我们的对话有时候是这样的：

我说："我要给我妈妈打电话。"（I am going to call my mother.）

他答："你要怎么称呼她？"（What are you going to call her?）

我问："我看上去怎么样？"（How do I look?）

他答："用眼睛。"（With your eyes.）

我问过很多英国人，想知道他们心目中的幽默是怎样的。可每个人的答案都不尽相同，甚至有人根本答不出来。正如我们中国的古代诗词和现代的新成语，大都是只能意会而不能言传的。

很久以前一个朋友送了我一本书，是 Bill Bryson 的 *Neither Here Nor There*。Bill虽然不是在英国出生的，但他在英国安家，有个英国太太和四个孩子。他书中的英式幽默我倒是很喜欢。那本书叙述了他在欧洲的一次游历。他是这么描写公共汽车的椅子的："The seats were designed by a dwarf seeking revenge on full-sized people."（这些座位是一个侏儒为了报复正常人而设计的。）他这样打发等待北极光的无聊时间：

Never had I slept so long and so well. Never had I this kind of leisure just to potter about. Suddenly I had time to do all kinds of things: unlace my boots and redo them over and over until the laces were precisely the same length, rearrange the contents of my wallet, deal with nose hairs, make long lists of all the things I would do if I had anything to do...

我从来没睡得这么好这么久过，我从来没有过如此无所事事的悠闲时光。突然间我有时间做各种各样的事情了：拆开我的皮靴上的鞋带并一次又一次的重新系上，直到鞋带两边的长度正好精确的一致；重新整理钱包里的东西；处理鼻毛；把我要做的事列出长长的清单（如果我有任何事情可做的话）。

他这么说米兰（其实他是在反讽意大利人的一些习惯）：

After southern Italy, Milan seemed hardly Italian at all. People walked quickly and purposefully... They didn't engage in passionate arguments about trivialities. They took meetings. They made deals. They drove with restraint, and parked neatly...

在意大利南部转了一圈之后来到米兰，发现米兰似乎完全不像意大利的城市。人们匆匆忙忙地行走，并且是有目的地行走……他们并不热衷于争辩细碎琐事。他们开会处理公事，他们做成生意也正儿八经的。他们有秩序有节制地开车，并且停车也停得干净利落……

以上内容引自 <http://bbs.cn.yahoo.com/message/read_-b3ZlcnNlYXM=_313797.html>

Detailed Notes to the Text（课文详解）

1. I supposed that the old lady in the flat above ours was moving the furniture about.

flat 名词，在此意为"公寓"，为英式英语用法，美式英语为 apartment。

above 在此为介词，意为"在……上方"，和 below 相对。例如：

We flew above the clouds.

我们在云层上飞行。

They lived in a flat above the shop.

他们住在商店上面的公寓内。

about 在此为副词，意为"到处，四处（活动）"。例如：

I am used to going about alone.

我习惯于一个人走来走去。

The little boy ran about looking for his mother.

小男孩四处跑着找妈妈。

Don't rush about.

别到处乱跑。

2. ... but I could see smoke coming through the letter box and under the door, and could smell something burning.

see smoke coming 是带现在分词的复合结构。例如：

I am glad to see you all looking so happy.

看到你们都很快乐，我真高兴。

Then he saw Laura coming up the street.

然后他看见罗拉从街那头过来。

I saw Dad mowing in the garden yesterday.

昨天我看见爸爸在花园除草。

smell something burning 中 smell 表示"闻到（某种味道），闻出"，它可用于引申意义，表示"感觉出"。例如：

Can you smell the smoke?

你能闻到烟味吗？

Do you smell something burning?

你闻到有东西烧着了的味道吗？

I smell something funny about the plan.

我觉察到这个计划有点可笑。

I could smell trouble coming.

我感到要有麻烦。

3. ... but the old lady took a long time to answer.

take 在此表示"需要花时间干某事"。例如：

It takes a lifetime to master dramatic form.

需要花上毕生的时间才能掌握戏剧形式。

It didn't take Jimmie very long to figure out the situation.

吉米没花多少时间就把情况弄明白了。

Writing books must take a great deal of time.

写书要花大量的时间。

4. ... when the water heater in the kitchen blew up.

blow up 在此意为"爆炸，炸毁"。例如：

The bomb blew up.

炸弹爆炸了。

The railway track was blown up at several strategic points.

在几个战略要点，铁轨都被炸了。

blow up 还表示"责骂，发火"。例如：

You are sure to be blown up for coming late to your work.

你上班迟到肯定会被批评。

When his secretary asked for the day off, Mr. Smith blew up.

当秘书要求请一天假时，史密斯先生发火了。

Her father blew up when she arrived home in the morning.

当她早晨回到家时，她爸爸发火了。

5. ... she said, looking embarrassed.

embarrass 意为"使发窘，使尴尬"。句中 embarrassed 为过去分词作表语。例如：

She was embarrassed at such a request.

对于这样的要求她感到很尴尬。

Arthur seemed embarrassed by the question.

这个问题使阿瑟感到很窘。

6. ... and the heater was in flames.

in flames 表示"燃烧着，在火中"。例如：

The house was in flames.

房子着火了。

7. ... You turned up promptly, I must say.

turn up 是动词 turn 的一种习惯用法。turn up 在句中的意思为"出现"。例如：

The missing boy turned up an hour later.

走失的男孩一小时后出现了。

Don't bother to look for my umbrella; it will turn up some day.

别费神找我的伞了，说不定哪天它自己就会出现的。

A man without training works at whatever jobs turn up.

没有接受过培训的人只能是碰上什么就干什么。

它还可表示"（声音）开大，（数额）增长"。例如：

Could you turn the music up?

你能把音乐开大点吗？

Investment is turning up sharply.

投资额在迅速增长。

8. It turned out that the fire was not very serious...

turn out 也是动词 turn 的一种习惯用法。在句中的意思为"结果是……，最后情况是……"。

1) 后面加从句。例如：

It turned out that he was George's father.

原来他是乔治的父亲。

It turns out that this method does not work well.

结果这个方法不怎么有效。

2) 后面加形容词或副词。例如：

It was cloudy this morning, but it turned out fine.

早上多云，但后来转晴了。

The examination turned out easy.

结果是这次考试很容易。

I was afraid things weren't going to turn out smooth for you.

我担心事情最后对你不利。

3) 后面加不定式 to be。例如：

Our meeting turned out to be interesting.

结果我们的聚会很有趣。

The letter turned out to be a forgery.

结果是那封信是伪造的。

9. ... my wife went up with the old lady to help her clear up the mess.

clear up 是 clear 的一种习惯用法，在句中表示"整理，收拾"。例如：

You'll have to clear up the things on the table before we have tea.

我们喝茶前你们该把桌子收拾干净。

Your desk is covered with papers; clear it up before you leave the office.

你的书桌上放满了文件，整理好再离开办公室。

I spent nearly an hour clearing up the room after the children's party.

孩子们聚会后我差不多花了一小时才把屋子收拾干净。

clear up 还表示"晴朗起来，开朗起来"。例如：

Now it is clearing up, and a sparrow is beginning to chirp.

天变得晴朗了，一只麻雀开始唧唧喳喳地叫。

The weather has cleared up; we can go out now.

天晴了，我们可以出去了。

Her face cleared up as she read the document.

读文件的时候，她的脸明朗了起来。

clear up 还可表示"澄清，使清楚，解决"。例如：

I'd like to clear up two or three points.

我想要澄清两三点。

The book has cleared up many difficulties for me.

这本书帮我弄清了很多难点。

As soon as the matter is cleared up, I shall write to you.

一旦事情搞清楚我就写信给你。

Key to Exercises（参考答案）

1. 1) His wife was afraid that the noise would wake the baby.

   2) The author could see smoke coming through the letter box and under the door, and could smell something burning.

   3) She was getting dressed.

   4) His wife was making the old lady a cup of tea.

   5) Because water was dripping slowly from the ceiling and forming a pool on the floor.

   6) Yes, he did.

   7) She was having a bath.

   8) No, she didn't.

   9) His wife went up with the old lady to help her clear up the mess.

   10) No, the baby woke up at last and started to cry after the baby heard the mother's scream.

2. 1) pour   2) returned   3) put out   4) take   5) Move
   6) watch   7) burn   8) made   9) forms   10) clear up

3. A. 1) B   2) A   3) D   4) C   5) C
      6) D   7) A   8) B   9) B   10) D

   B. 1) A   2) C   3) B   4) A   5) D
      6) C   7) A   8) C   9) D   10) B
      11) C   12) C   13) C   14) B   15) D

4. 1) B   2) A   3) A   4) A   5) D
   6) A   7) D   8) B   9) C   10) C

5. A. 1) He turned down the TV.

     2) Please shut the door.

     3) Somebody is knocking at the door.

     4) I have already turned off the gas.

     5) The foreign friends will arrive in Beijing tomorrow morning.

     6) This is a very serious fire.

     7) We must do our best to prevent fire.

     8) My daughter woke up suddenly at midnight yesterday.

     9) Please go upstairs!

    10) All of us visited the exhibition except him.

   B. 1) 我读书，她看电视。

     2) 我可以看见烟从信箱里和门底下冒出来，并且闻到了东西燃烧的气味。

     3) 我正想着要去砸门时，她终于露面了。

     4) 你敲门时，我正在穿衣服。

     5) 烟从厨房里冒出来，热水器在燃烧。

     6) 当我回到家时，我妻子正为老太太沏茶。

     7) 他们走后，妻子和老太太一同上楼去帮她清理房间。

     8) 除了加热器外，没有任何东西受损。

     9) 幸好孩子没有被这吵闹声弄醒！

    10) 当我赶到那里时，发现水正从天花板上慢慢地滴落下来，并且在地上形成了一个水洼。

6. 1) C   2) D   3) C   4) C   5) D
   6) B   7) C   8) A   9) B   10) A

Reading:

1. 1) C   2) C   3) B   4) C   5) A

2. 1) T   2) F   3) T   4) F   5) T

Listening:

1. M: Have you heard what George has been saying about your work?

   W: Yes, I have, but I could't care less.

   Q: What does the woman mean by her remark?

2. W: Mary seems happy with her new job.

   M: Happy? She's thinking of giving it up.

   Q: How does Mary like her present job?

3. W: I hear it's going to snow this afternoon.

   M: Going to snow? The ground is already wet.

   Q: What can we learn from the man's reply?

4. M: I hear you are moving to a new apartment next week.

   W: Yes, my roommate plays the radio all night and I can't sleep well.

   Q: Why is the woman going to move?

5. M: Jane, you seem to have worked overtime at your office.

   W: That is true. But I don't mind the extra hours, because the work is interesting.

   Q: What does the woman think of her work?

Key:

1. A   2. A   3. B   4. C   5. A

Dictation:

On the evening of June 21st, 1992, a tall man with brown hair and blue eyes entered the beautiful hall of the Bell Tower Hotel in Xi'an with his bicycle. The hotel workers received him and telephoned the manager, for they had never seen a bicycle in the hotel hall before though they lived in the kingdom of bicycles.

Robert Friedlander, an American, arrived in Xi'an on his bicycle trip across Asia which started last December in New Delhi, India.

When he was 11, he read a book about Marco Polo and made up his mind to visit the Silk Road. Now, after 44 years, he was on the Silk Road in Xi'an and his early dreams were coming true.

Chinese Translation （课文参考译文）

着火了！着火了！

上周的一个晚上，我和妻子静静地坐在家里。我读书，她看电视。突然，我们听到砰的一声巨响。我猜想可能是我们楼上的老太太在搬家具。妻子担心声音太大会把孩子吵醒。她将电视的声音调低。不一会儿，我们听到有人呼喊求救。

我跑上楼。老太太的门关着。但是我可以看到烟从信箱里和门底下冒出来，并闻到了东西燃烧的气味。我向楼下朝妻子大声喊到："她家着火了。快给消防队打电话。"

我用力敲门，但是老太太好半天才答应。我正想着要去砸门时，她终于露面了。

她说："我洗澡时厨房加热器爆炸了。"

我问她："你为什么不开门呢?"

她不好意思地说："你敲门时，我正在穿衣服。"

我把她送到我们家。然后，我又跑回到老太太家里，关了煤气以防再度爆炸。烟从厨房里冒出来，加热器在燃烧。正在这时，外面传来消防车的警笛声和消防队员上楼时沉重的脚步声。我转过身，看到两个消防队员站在门口。

"就是这儿。"我说。"我得说，你们来得正是时候。"

当我回到家时，我妻子正在为老太太沏茶。不一会儿，消防队长来询问一些问题。幸好，火势并不严重，已被消防队员扑灭。他们走后，妻子和老太太一起上楼去帮她清理房间。

妻子回来时说："没事儿了。除了加热器外，没有任何东西受损。幸好孩子没被这吵闹声弄醒!"

她将茶杯拿到厨房。此时，我听到她的尖叫和杯子掉到地上的声音。当我赶到那里时，发现水正在从天花板上慢慢地滴落下来，并且在地上形成了一个水洼。孩子终于醒了，大哭起来。

UNIT 6 *Memory*

Background Knowledge（背景知识）

我们通常采用以下几种方式对记忆进行分类。

1. 按记忆时启动的主要人体感官划分：

（1）视觉记忆	（2）听觉记忆	（3）嗅觉记忆
（4）味觉记忆	（5）触觉记忆	（6）平衡觉记忆
（7）视听觉结合记忆	（8）视听触觉结合记忆	（9）多种感觉器官结合记忆

2. 按记忆的材料在脑中保持的时间划分：

（1）瞬时记忆

又称感觉记忆，保持时间不超过一秒钟，瞬现即逝、须臾即忘，人们往往感觉不到。大脑对此类信息不作加工和重复，形成的痕迹是浅表而活动的，一秒钟以后就消失，遗忘后不能恢复。

（2）短时记忆

也叫操作记忆，保持时间大于一秒但不超过一两分钟，常和一定的操作动作相联系，操作结束，准确的记忆内容也就消失。边记边忘的短时记忆是一种正常现象，能减轻大脑的记忆负担。

（3）长时记忆

保持时间大于一两分钟，通常能保持较长时间，有的可终生不忘。大脑对此类信息进行了储存前的主动、积极加工，形成的痕迹大都是结构的、深刻的、牢固的，保持时间较长，遗忘后大都能回想起来。

同一内容经过反复记忆，可以延长记忆时间，把短时记忆转化为长时记忆。动物实验结果表明，记忆痕迹在受试老鼠的脑中至少要持续 90 秒钟，短时记忆才会转变而巩固为长时记忆。对人类则只需四五秒钟。

3. 按记忆材料的大脑半球划分：

（1）左半球记忆：负责记忆逻辑信息和语言信息

（2）右半球记忆：负责记忆形象信息和艺术信息

此外，人们还从心理特征方面将记忆划分为情绪记忆和非情绪记忆；按照生理特征将记忆划分为运动记忆和非运动记忆等。

Detailed Notes to the Text（课文详解）

1. Memorize these words.

memorize *vt.* 记忆

You'd better memorize these important telephone numbers.

你最好记住这些重要的电话号码。

They are also beginning the task of memorizing the dialogue.

他们也开始了背诵那段对话的任务。

2. You remember thing every day,...

every day *adv.* 每天

everyday *adj.* 每天的

He calls his mother every day.

他每天都给母亲打电话。

You must come to see me every day.

你必须每天都来看我。

Don't be too upset. These are just the problems of everyday life.

不要太难过，这些问题是我们日常生活中难免要遇到的。

Cooking breakfast is an everyday job.

做早饭是一项每天要做的事。

People liked the book, because it was about their everyday life.

人们喜欢这本书是因为它讲述的是人们的日常生活。

3. It lasts less than 30 seconds.

1) **last** *vi.* 持续；耐用，耐穿

A good coat will last you ten years.

一件好大衣能穿十年。

2) **less than...** 少于

more than... 多于，超过

It was more than a year now since he had seen her.

自从他上次见到她已经一年多了。

We advertised for pupils last autumn, and got more than 60.

我们去年秋天作广告招收学生，结果招收了 60 多个。

More than ten thousand workers were involved in the strike.

有一万多名工人参加了罢工。

He can't be more than thirty.

他超不过 30 岁。

There are more than forty students in our class.

我们班有 40 多个学生。

4. You did not learn it in the beginning.

in the beginning 在开始时，起初

at the beginning of 在……初（指时间）；在……开头（指位置）

In the beginning some of us took no interest in it.

起初我们有些人对它不感兴趣。

In the beginning there were no men, nor animals, nor plants.

起初没有人类，也没有动物和植物。

At the beginning of August an event occurred.

八月初发生了一件事情。

This adverb can also be placed at the beginning of the sentence.

这个副词也可以放在句首。

5. This is the major reason for forgetting.

1) **major** *adj.* 主要的

This is the major reason for your failure.

这是你失败的主要原因。

I think that you have been wrong on all major issues.

我认为在主要问题上你一直是错的。

2) **reason for (doing) sth.** （做）某事的原因

Is this the only reason for learning English?

这是学英语的唯一理由吗？

Sickness was the reason for Mary's absence.

玛丽缺席是因为她生病了。

6. Spend time on it.

spend + time/money + on + *n.* 在……上花费时间或金钱

She spends a lot of money on clothes.

她花很多钱买衣服。

He spends more time on sports than on studies.

他花在体育运动上的时间比花在学习上的多。

7. It is difficult to memorize something you don't understand.

It is + *adj.* + to do sth. 是 it 的一个用法，在这种结构中，it 本身并没有任何实在的意思，它只是一个形式主语，to do sth. 才是真正的主语。使用这个结构往往是因为主语过长，如果按照惯例将 to do sth. 放在句首的话，整个句子会显得头重脚轻，失去平衡。

It is useful to know a foreign language.

掌握一门外语是很有用的。

It is not easy to finish the work in two days.

在两天内完成这项工作不是一件容易的事。

8. When you learn the word SOFA, make a picture in your mind of this furniture.

注意 furniture 是不可数名词。例如：

They had bought some furniture in London, mostly second-hand.

他们已经在伦敦买了一些家具，大都是二手的。

This old French table is a very valuable piece of furniture.

这张旧式法国桌子是件很值钱的家具。

We have lots of pieces of furniture in our house.

我们的房子里有很多家具。

Some articles of furniture were lost when we moved.

我们搬家时丢了几件家具。

9. Remember what it looks like.

look like 看上去像；长得像

Tom looks like a movie star.

汤姆长得像一个电影明星。

The book looks like a dictionary.

这本书像本词典。

10. Try to relax when you study.

relax *vt.* 放松

A hot bath should help to relax you.

洗个热水澡有助于让你放松下来。

Forget your worries and relax.

忘却烦恼，放松下来。

Key to Exercises（参考答案）

1. 1) Short-term memory and photographic memory.

   2) Less than 30 seconds.

   3) Long-term memory.

   4) Long-term memory has everything that one remembers.

   5) Because we didn't learn it in the beginning.

   6) Practise the information. Spend time on it.

   7) No, of course not.

   8) Do not have more than seven parts of information.

   9) Learn one part and stop for a few minutes. Don't try to learn all parts at the same time.

   10) No, we can't.

2. A. 1) be divided into

   2) in the beginning

   3) connected with

   4) Be sure that

   5) at one time

   6) spend on

   7) At the beginning of

   8) major

   9) last

   10) at a time

   B. 1) Although/Though

   2) no matter what / whatever

   3) as

   4) Whoever

   5) even if

   6) Whatever / No matter what

   7) no matter how / however

   8) Even if

   9) Even though

   10) no matter how / however

3. 1) D   2) C   3) D   4) D   5) C

   6) D   7) A   8) A   9) B   10) A

11) B	12) A	13) A	14) B	15) B
16) B	17) D	18) C	19) D	20) C
21) C	22) C	23) D	24) D	25) B
26) A	27) A	28) D	29) C	30) D

4. A. 1) Our English teacher told us to memorize these words.

2) I see him every day.

3) They only offered a few common everyday expressions.

4) The hot weather lasted for the whole month of July.

5) He lives on less than five hundred dollars a month.

6) You will find it rather difficult in the beginning.

7) You'll find the sentence at the beginning of the chapter.

8) Parking is one of the major problems in London.

9) At a time like this I don't grudge a thing.

10) He looks like his mother.

B. 1) 把你的短时记忆转变为长时记忆。

2) 你在电话簿上查到了一个电话号码，拨完之后就把它忘记了。这是你的短时记忆，它持续的时间不足 30 秒。

3) 你的长时记忆中储存着你记住的一切。

4) 从一开始你就没有把它记住。

5) 你很难记住你不理解的信息。

6) 一心不可二用。

7) 努力把新的信息与你已知的信息联系起来。

8) 把信息分成若干部分，但最多不得超过 7 个部分。

9) 在脑中勾画出一个图像。

10) 有些人具有图片式的记忆本领。

5. 1) B   2) A   3) C   4) D   5) B

   6) A   7) B   8) A   9) C   10) B

6.

American Toy Company

Dear Sir or Madam,

I saw the advertisement of your company in *Business Week* the other day, and I want to apply for the position of a salesman in your organization. I am 24 years old, and can speak English and Cantonese. I am rich in commercial knowledge, skillful at sale, and have good relation with local salesmen selling toys. If I can be employed, I am sure that I could increase the amount of toys to be sold. References are available upon request.

Yours faithfully,
Wang Lin

Reading:

1. 1) C   2) D   3) C   4) A   5) B

2. 1) T   2) T   3) F   4) T   5) T

Listening:

1. M: I think I should call him up and ask him if it's OK.

   W: You'd better do it right away.

   Q: When should the man call him according to the woman?

2. M: Should I call an ambulance?

   W: No, no. That's OK.

   Q: Why is it not necessary for the man to call an ambulance?

3. M: What time are we supposed to be there?

   W: By ten o'clock.

   Q: When should they get there?

4. M: We can't park here.

   W: Only five minutes.

   Q: How long can they park here?

5. M: So tell me about your new job. How is it going?

   W: I'm working as a waitress.

   M: That sounds like a hard job. Do you have to work long hours?

   W: Well, I work at lunch time, and sometimes in the evening until 11.

   M: How many days a week?

   W: I have to do six shifts a week; it's quite a lot.

   M: I'll never see you then. Do you have any days off?

   W: Don't worry. I don't have to work every weekend.

   Q: How many days a week does the woman have to work?

Key:

1. A   2. B   3. C   4. D   5. B

Dictation:

Not all people like to work, but everyone likes to play. All over the world men and women and boys and girls enjoy sports. Since ancient times, adults and children have called their friends together to spend hours, even days, playing games.

Sports help people to live happily. They help to keep people healthy and feeling good. When they are playing games, people move a lot. This is good for their health. Having fun with their friends makes them happy.

Chinese Translation （课文参考译文）

记忆

"记住这些单词。""掌握这个拼写规则。""不要忘记明天的测验。"你每天都需要记忆一些东西，但你又是如何将它们记住的呢？

你在电话簿上查到了一个电话号码，拨完之后就把它忘了。这是你的短时记忆，它持续的时间不足 30 秒。但是你不会到电话簿上查找最要好的朋友的电话号码，因为你已经记住了。这是你的长时记忆。你的长时记忆中储存着你记住的一切。

为什么有些事情你会遗忘呢？这是什么原因呢？这是因为从一开始你就没有把它记住。这就是遗忘的主要原因。但是你还是能够记忆得更好一些的。以下教你一些记忆方法。

1. 把你的短时记忆转变为长时记忆。花一些功夫，练习这些信息。

2. 务必要理解这些信息。你很难记住你不理解的东西。

3. 一心不可二用。选择一个安静的场所学习。听音乐和记住东西是无法同时进行的。

4. 努力把新的信息与你已知的信息联系起来。

5. 把信息分成若干部分，但不得多于 7 个部分。学习一部分然后休息几分钟。不要试图把所有的部分同时记住。

6. 在脑中勾画出一个图像。例如，当你学习 sofa 这个词时，在大脑中想象这件家具的样子，记住它的外观。

7. 在学习时尽量放松，把学习当作一种享受。疲劳或心情不好时你是记不住东西的。

有些人具有图片式的记忆本领。他们看任何东西都像是看一张图片。这样，他们能够记住很多东西。你想具有这种图片式记忆能力吗？

UNIT 7 *Oil*

Background Knowledge (背景知识)

石油又称原油，是从地下深处开采的棕黑色可燃黏稠液体。石油是古代海洋或湖泊中的生物经过漫长的演化形成的混合物，与煤一样属于化石燃料。石油的性质因产地而异，密度为 0.8~1.0 克 / 厘米³，黏度范围很宽，凝固点差别很大（30~-60℃），沸点范围为常温到 500℃ 以上，可溶于多种有机溶剂，不溶于水，但可与水形成乳状液。组成石油的化学元素主要是碳（83%~87%）、氢（11%~14%），其余为硫（0.06%~0.8%）、氮（0.02%~1.7%）、氧（0.08%~1.82%）及微量金属元素（镍、钒、铁等）。由碳和氢化合形成的烃类构成石油的主要组成部分，约占 95%~99%，含硫、氧、氮的化合物对石油产品有害，在石油加工中应尽量除去。

石油的发现、开采和直接利用由来已久。加工利用并逐渐形成石油炼制工业始于 19 世纪 30 年代，到 20 世纪 40~50 年代形成的现代炼油工业，是最大的加工工业之一。19 世纪 30 年代起，陆续建立了石油蒸馏工厂，产品主要是灯用煤油，汽油没有用途当废料抛弃。19 世纪 70 年代建造了润滑油厂，并开始把蒸馏得到的高沸点油做锅炉燃料。19 世纪末内燃机的问世使汽油和柴油的需求猛增，仅靠原油的蒸馏（即原油的一次加工）不能满足需求，于是诞生了以增产汽、柴油为目的，综合利用原油各种成分的原油二次加工工艺。如 1913 年实现了热裂化，1930 年实现了焦化，1930 年实现了催化裂化，1940 年实现了催化重整，此后加氢技术也迅速发展，这就形成了现代的石油炼制工业。20 世纪 50 年代以后，石油炼制为化工产品的发展提供了大量原料，形成了现代的石油化学工业。

（摘自中国能源信息网 http://www.nengyuan.net）

▶ Detailed Notes to the Text （课文详解）

1. Great quantities of animal oil come from whales, the largest remaining animals in the world.

这里的 the largest remaining animals in the world 与 whales 是同位语关系。例如：

John, Tom's father, is an engineer.

约翰，汤姆的父亲，是一名工程师。

quantity 数量（可用作可数名词）。例如：

He buys things in large quantities.

他经常大量购物。

What quantity can be supplied?

供给量可能会有多大？

I have quantities of good clothes.

我有很多好衣服。

remaining *adj.* "余下的；剩余的"，这个形容词只做定语，即只能修饰名词，而不能用做表语。例如：

The only remaining question is whether we can take a holiday somewhere.

唯一剩下的问题是我们能否去什么地方度假。

The remaining students will serve as the audience.

剩余的学生将会去做观众。

2. ..., the blubber is stripped off and boiled down, either aboard or on shore.

either... or... （二者中）或是……或是；不是……就是……。例如：

Either your mother or your father, or both parents may go with you.

或是你父亲，或是你母亲，或者你父母双方可以与你一同前往。

Either the shirts or the sweater is a good buy.

这些衬衫或这件毛衣都挺便宜，值得买。

注意：either... or 连接主语时，谓语动词的单复数取决于 or 后面的名词，这点从上面的第三个例句就可以看出。

on shore 在岸上，在陆上。例如：

We had a couple of hours on shore.

我们在岸上呆了两个小时左右。

When the ship reached the port, the passengers were allowed to go on shore.

轮船到港后，乘客方可登岸。

3. Some of the Indians of North America used to collect and sell the oil from the wells of Pennsylvania.

used to do sth. 过去常常做某事，含有"现在已不做了"的意味。例如：

He used to get up early.

他过去常早起。

We used to grow beautiful roses.

我们过去曾经种植非常漂亮的玫瑰花。

I get on well with him nowadays. Better than I used to.

我现在和他相处得很好，比以前好。

4. No household can get on without it.

get on 过日子；生活下去。例如：

You can't get on without money in this world.

在这个世界上，没有钱是无法生存的。

How would you get on without me?

没有我你怎么生活呢？

How will Mr. Andrews get on without a housekeeper?

没有管家，安德鲁先生将如何生活呢？

5. When engineers refer to oil, they always mean…, the oil that is used to lubricate all kinds of machinery.

refer to

(1) 指……而言，指的是。例如：

By "teacher" we refer to the person who supplies the information.

说到"老师"，我们是指提供信息的人。

What do these words in brackets refer to?

那括号里的字是指什么？

(2) 查阅，参考。例如：

For information about trains you must refer to a timetable.

要了解火车的信息，你必须查阅列车时刻表。

Please refer to the last page of the book for answers.

请查阅本书的最后一页寻找答案。

lubricate *vt.* 使润滑。例如：

This oil lubricates the machine.

这种油能够润滑机器。

You should lubricate the wheels of your bicycle once a month.

你应该一个月给你的自行车轱辘上一次油。

After washing your hands, you'd better lubricate them with hand lotion.

洗完手后，你最好用护手霜滋润一下。

6. ..., the oil became of world-wide importance.

of importance (= important) 重要的。例如：

Knowing a foreign language is of great importance.

懂一门外语是非常重要的。

Healthy diet is of importance.

健康的饮食很重要。

This matter is of great/no/not much/little importance.

这件事情非常 / 不 / 不太 / 一点不重要。

Key to Exercises（参考答案）

1.
1) Great quantities of animal oil come from whales.

2) Whales are the largest remaining animals in the world.

3) Because whales live in the Arctic seas; to protect them from the cold there, nature has provided them with a thick covering of fat.

4) Blubber.

5) Vegetable oil has been known from ancient times.

6) Perfumes may be made from the oils of certain flowers.

7) Mineral oil can be used to drive cars, airplanes and locomotives, and it can also be used to lubricate all kinds of machinery.

8) Mineral oil has changed the life of the common man.

9) People did not seem to have realized the importance of mineral oil until it was found that paraffin-oil could be made from it.

10) The appearance of paraffin-oil led to the development of the wells and to the making of enormous profits.

2.
1) strip off	2) lead to
3) getting on	4) provides... with
5) quantity	6) is made from
7) lubricated	8) refer to
9) protect... from	10) make profits

3. A. 1) D   2) D   3) C   4) C   5) D

     6) D   7) A   8) B   9) A   10) B

11) D	12) B	13) C	14) B	15) B
16) A	17) B	18) D	19) B	20) C
21) C	22) C	23) C	24) A	25) C
26) C	27) A	28) D	29) C	30) C

| B. 1) A | 2) B | 3) A | 4) B | 5) C |
| 6) A | 7) A | 8) B | 9) A | 10) C |

4. A. 1) This hotel buys a large quantity of meat every day.

2) You can come either today or tomorrow.

3) They stay in a small wood house on shore.

4) If only you'd be as you used to be!

5) He was wearing dark glasses to protect his eyes from the sun.

6) Was he able to provide you with the information?

7) How would you get on without me?

8) A person refers to a dictionary, mainly, to find the meanings of words.

9) If I have improved in any way, I owe it all to you.

10) The incident led to his resignation.

B. 1) 大量的动物油来自鲸——世界上现存的最大的动物。

2) 为了使鲸免受北极的严寒，大自然赋予了鲸一层厚厚的被称为鲸脂的脂肪。

3) 当鲸被杀死后，鲸脂在船上或在岸上被剥离并加以熬炼。

4) 没有油，一家人就无法生活，因为烹饪离不开油。

5) 当工程师们说起油时，他们一般指矿物油，即用来开汽车、飞机和火车的油，用来润滑机器的油。

6) 是这种油改变了大众的生活。

7) 有了这种油，才出现了汽车。有了这种油，才使飞行成为可能。

8) 油井存在的历史已经非常久远了。

9) 然而在发现能从这种油中提取出煤油以前，似乎没有人认识到它的重要性。这一发现促进了油井的发展并带来了巨额利润。

10) 当内燃机发明之后，这种油具有了世界范围的重要性。

| 5. 1) B | 2) A | 3) D | 4) A | 5) C |
| 6) B | 7) C | 8) D | 9) A | 10) B |

69

Reading:

1. 1) A   2) C   3) B   4) D   5) B

2. 1) F   2) F   3) T   4) T   5) T

Listening:

1. M: Do you mind if I open the window?

   W: Of course not. It is so hot today.

   Q: What does the man want to do?

2. M: Could I read your newspaper for a while?

   W: No problem.

   Q: Is it OK for the man to read the woman's newspaper?

3. M: May I borrow your umbrella?

   W: I am sorry. This is the only umbrella I have.

   Q: Why doesn't the woman lend the man her umbrella?

4. M: Are we permitted to take pictures here?

   W: Sorry, I am a stranger here, too.

   Q: According to the woman, can the man take a picture there?

5. M: Would it be all right if I change the channel?

   W: Go ahead, please.

   Q: Can the man change the channel?

Key:

1. A   2. B   3. B   4. D   5. C

Dictation:

     The elephant is the only animal in the world with a trunk. It uses its trunk in many ways. It pulls leaves off trees with its trunk and then puts them into its mouth. It also uses its trunk to get water. The trunk can hold a lot of water, as an elephant needs to drink more than three hundred pints of water every day.

     When an elephant is angry, its tusks can be very dangerous. The tusks of an elephant are really its front teeth. People pay a lot of money for the ivory of an elephant's tusks. In Africa men have hunted elephants for their tusks. The ivory from the tusks is made into many beautiful things. But now the practice is banned as it should be for being so cruel.

Chinese Translation（课文参考译文）

油

油主要分成三大类：动物油、植物油和矿物油。大量的动物油来自鲸——世界上现存的最大的动物。为了使鲸免受北极的严寒，大自然赋予了它一层厚厚的被称为鲸脂的脂肪。当鲸被杀死后，鲸脂在船上或在岸上被剥离并加以熬炼。鲸脂生产出大量的油，用来制造供人类消费的食品。

古代就已有了植物油。没有油，一家人就无法生活，因为烹饪离不开油。某些鲜花中的油可以提炼出香水。肥皂也是由植物油和动物油制成的。

当工程师们说起油时，他们一般指矿物油，即用来开汽车、飞机和火车的油，用来润滑机器的油。是这种油改变了大众的生活。有了这种油，才出现了汽车。有了这种油，才使飞行成为可能。这种油来自地下。

从很久以前人们就知道油井的存在。北美印第安人过去曾从宾夕法尼亚州的油井收集并出售这种油。然而直到发现能从这种油中提取出煤油，人们才认识到它的重要性。这一发现促进了油井的发展并带来了巨额利润。当内燃机发明之后，这种油具有了世界范围的重要性。

UNIT 8 *Crazy About Animals*

Background Knowledge (背景知识)

英国是动物保护工作起步最早，动物保护工作比较完善的国家。在英国，不论大小动物，不论家畜还是野生动物，都受动物保护法的保护。最早的动物保护法是 1911 年颁布的，之后有九个相关的修正案和补充条款，分别对处罚力度和适用范围加以调整，同时还针对某些特种动物，比如马、牛、以及用于商业用途或屠宰的动物，作出特别规定。这一整套法律目前仍适用，具体情况如下：

● Protection of Animals Act 1911

这是最早制定的法律，也是最重要的法规，规定了主要以下几个方面：

1. "虐待动物罪"（"Offence of Cruelty to Animals"）的定义，以及相应的处罚和量刑。

2. 法院有权剥夺动物所有人对被虐待动物的所有权，并有权在兽医的建议下决定是否处死动物，以避免动物继续遭受无法治愈的痛苦。

3. 虐待动物的人必须对其虐待行为对动物所有人产生的损失进行赔偿（根据英国判例法，这里的损失应该也包括精神损害）。

4. 在公路上利用狗协助拉车或任何载具的将被处以罚款。

5. 如果兽医认为受伤的动物继续存活将不可避免地遭受痛苦折磨，警察在兽医的建议下，可以对受伤的动物在其动物所有人不在场的情况下决定处死该动物。如果兽医认为无需处死该动物，动物所有人必须在警察的监督下带走该受伤动物，并予以医治。若所有人不从，警察可以自行决定带走受伤动物进行医治，并且由法院判决所有人承担一切费用。如果所有人拒绝承担，即被判定藐视法庭，在英国最高刑期可以达到 3 年。

6. 即使是为了人类的食物而对动物进行屠宰，也不得对动物造成任何不必要的痛苦，否则该法律对屠宰人以及动物所有人也适用。

7. 除了农业上为了消灭害虫的合理使用外，禁止贩卖、分发有毒的谷物，种子，或者在土地或建筑物内施放其他任何毒药，毒液或者有毒食物，否则处以罚款。

● Protection of Animals Act (Amendment Act) 1912

这是 1912 年的修正案，主要是把虐待动物罪的刑期从 3 个月提升到 6 个月监禁。

● Protection of Animals Act (Amendment Act) 1921

这是 1921 年的修正案，对该法律所不适用的围猎行为进行修改。

● Protection of Animals Act (Amendment Act) 1927

这是 1927 年的修正案，对投毒的规定的例外条款进行修改。

- Protection of Animals Act (Amendment Act) 1934

1934 年的修正案，主要加入了禁止用绳索套住未经训练的马匹或公牛（就像美国牛仔玩的那种游戏），鞭打、殴打马匹、牛以及公开进行与马匹或者牛有关的并带有虐待意味的表演等行为的规定。

- Protection of Animals Act (Amendment Act) 1954

1954 年的修正案增加了法院的权力。法院有权剥夺犯有虐待动物罪的人今后在一定期限内饲养动物的权利，并且增加了罚款的数额。

- Protection of Animals (Penalties) Act 1987

1987 年的修正案大幅增加了对虐待动物人的罚款上限，从 50 英镑增加到最高 5,000 英镑（相当于 6-7 万人民币）。

- Protection of Animals Act (Amendment Act) 1988

88 年修正案除了调整了 54 年修正案的剥夺饲养权利外，还增加了禁止利用动物打斗的行为，如斗鸡，斗狗等。

- Protection Against Cruel Tethering Act 1988

该法主要是限制不得对马匹、驴子、骡子进行可能对他们造成痛苦的束缚和圈养。

- Protection of Animals Act (Amendment Act) 2000

该法主要是对照顾、处置（包括贩卖）以及屠宰动物的一些行为加入了监督措施，以及赋予某些政府检控人员进入住宅，物业执法的权利。

总之，英国的动物保护法对虐待动物行为处罚是比较严厉的，可以处以 6 个月以下监禁，同时可以并处 5,000 英镑以下的罚款。虐待动物包括：

1. 残忍的殴打，脚踢，恶意对待，蹂躏，过度驱使，过度负重，折磨，激怒或者恐吓任何动物；或者作为动物所有人允许他人虐待自己的动物的行为；
2. 放任或者不合理的实施让动物遭受不必要的痛苦的行为；
3. 导致，获取或者协助动物打斗或者提供动物打斗场所的行为；
4. 故意，或者无合理理由对动物施于毒药或者导致伤害的物品的行为；
5. 其他对动物的不人道或没有合理措施的手术的行为。

Detailed Notes to the Text（课文详解）

1. They race them, catch them, train them and breed them.

race *vt.* 把……投入比赛

He will not race his dog this year because it is getting old.

他今年将不会让他的狗参赛，因为它老了。

He will be racing a Ferrari in this year's Formula One Championships.

在今年的一级方程式冠军赛中他将驾驶一辆法拉利参赛。

train sb. to do sth. 训练，培养

My parents trained me to behave properly.

我父母教育我要举止得体。

He must train the muscles of his tongue and lips to produce new sounds.

为了发出这个音，他必须训练他的舌头和唇部肌肉。

breed *vt.* 养殖，培育；教养，培养

Many farmers breed cows and sheep.

许多农场主养殖奶牛和绵羊。

He is a young man of modest breeding.

他是一个出身平常的年轻人。

2. Racing animals is another very popular activity.

racing animals 是动名词，在这里做主语，本课中类似的句子还有：

Looking after and **being kind** to animals is only one part of the story.

Catching and **hunting** them is another great British hobby.

3. Only the very rich can afford to keep and race their own.

afford *vt.*

1）和 can，could，be able to 联用，表示 "有时间或经济条件等做某事"

(1) 跟不定式

He was envious of his brother because he could afford to give so much.

他嫉妒他的哥哥，因为他出手阔绰。

We can't afford to pay such a big price.

我们付不起这么大价钱。

(2) 跟名词或代词

I can't afford so much money.

我付不起这么多钱。

I don't think we'll be able to afford any travel this year.

我认为我们今年根本没钱去任何地方旅游。

2）经得起（多跟不定式）

He cannot afford to offend his employer.

他得罪不起老板。

He could not afford to lose his fortune entirely.

他经受不起丧失所有财产。

4. Racehorse owners can be seen in their best clothes...

这里的 in 表示"穿着……"

She's in plain clothes.

她穿着普通。

Letty was in light blue silk.

莱迪身穿浅兰色丝绸衣服。

5. Millions of people like to spend their Saturdays and Sundays sitting quietly beside a lake or a river, waiting for a fish to bite.

spend...doing sth. 花（时间）做某事

She spent most of her free time watching TV.

她的大部分空余时间都用来看电视了。

We spent a whole day yesterday cleaning our office.

我们昨天花了一整天时间打扫办公室。

wait (for sb.) to do sth. 等待（某人）做某事

Dodge is waiting to have a word with you.

道奇正等着和你聊一聊。

I'm waiting to use that machine.

我在等用那台机器。

6. And a few people still enjoy hunting foxes, ...

enjoy doing sth. 喜欢做某事

Their children enjoy helping around the house.

他们的孩子非常喜欢帮父母做事。

I enjoy working with you very much.

我很喜欢和你一起工作。

Key to Exercises（参考答案）

1. 1) They race them, catch them, train them and breed them.

2) It could be a dog, a cat, or a goldfish.

3) Because they are lonely.

4) Racing pigeons is more common because only the very rich can afford to keep and race horses.

5) They are seen in their best clothes.

6) The Queen and the other members of the Royal Family.

7) They can afford to bet some money on the winners.

8) Whenever you are in Britain, you'll find a "betting shop" not very far away.

9) They catch and kill them. For example, they enjoy fishing, hunting foxes, or shooting deer, or catching rabbits.

10) "I can say anything I like to my cat, but she never thinks I'm silly."

2. 1) breed   2) are crazy about

   3) afford   4) are in their best clothes

   5) reserved, is different with   6) waiting for

   7) bet on   8) hobbies

   9) race   10) fancier

3. 1) C   2) B   3) C   4) D   5) C

   6) B   7) C   8) A   9) C   10) B

   11) B   12) D   13) A   14) D   15) A

   16) A   17) B   18) C   19) D   20) B

   21) A   22) A   23) D   24) B   25) B

   26) D   27) C   28) D   29) B   30) D

4. A. 1) shorter, shortest   2) brighter   3) coldest   4) wetter

     5) longer   6) bigger, biggest   7) softer, softest   8) hotter

     9) lighter   10) younger, youngest

     11) most considerate, more considerate   12) more peaceful, Most peaceful

     13) more serious   14) more famous, most famous

     15) more difficult, most difficult   16) more astonishing, most astonishing

     17) more ordinary, most ordinary   18) more thoughtful, most thoughtful

     19) more interesting, most interesting   20) most pleasant, more pleasant

5. A. 1) Of course she misses him. She is crazy about him.

     2) My boss races cars professionally.

     3) Chinese people have successfully bred pandas in Wolong National Natural Reserve.

     4) In this way we can train them to read fluently and accurately.

     5) I don't think we'll be able to afford any travel this year.

6) She was in a new black overcoat with a velvet collar.

7) She spent most of her free time watching TV.

8) Don't wait for us to join you at the table.

9) He enjoys doing something new.

10) A reserved person does not make friends easily.

B. 1) 他们喜欢从电视新闻节目中收听有关动物的故事，他们还喜欢阅读有关动物的书籍。

2) 一些孤独的老人喜欢他们的猫或狗，就如同喜欢他们的人类朋友一样。

3) 当动物爱好者去世时，他们会把钱留在"猫收容所"，"狗收容所"，或者是"老马收容所"。

4) 要赛鸽你不必很有钱，但要想赛马情形就不同了。

5) 只有那些特别有钱的人才养得起马，并让自己的马参加比赛。

6) 在重大赛事上，你能够看见赛马的主人们身着最漂亮的服装，同女王及皇室的其他成员们在一起。

7) 但是几乎所有的人都能赌马，并且很多人也是这样做的。

8) 无论在英国的什么地方，你都能在不远的地方找到一个"赛马赌注登记处"。

9) 照顾和善待动物只是人们喜爱动物的一种表现。

10) 数以万计的人喜欢在星期六和星期日静静地坐在湖边或河边等着鱼上钩。

6. 1) C   2) B   3) B   4) B   5) D

   6) C   7) A   8) D   9) B   10) A

7.

Dear Mr. and Mrs. Smith,

How time flies! It is a long time since we met last time. We miss you very much. We would like to invite you over to dinner at our home at 5 p.m. on June 23rd, Saturday. After dinner we will go to the concert together.

Best wishes! We are looking forward to seeing you then!

Yours sincerely,

Mr. and Mrs. Brown

Reading:

1. 1) B   2) C   3) A   4) B   5) A

2. 1) F   2) T   3) F   4) F   5) T

Listening:

1. M: Do you mind if I switch off the TV? It is so noisy.

   W: Of course not.

   Q: Why does the man want to turn off the TV?

2. M: Could I shut the door?

   W: No, you mustn't. It is so hot in here.

   Q: Why doesn't the woman agree to close the door?

3. M: May I use your dictionary?

   W: Yes, no problem.

   Q: What does the man want to use?

4. M: I want to go to the zoo tomorrow. Do you mind if I borrow your map?

   W: Not at all.

   Q: Where is the man going tomorrow?

5. M: May I use your telephone, please?

   W: Certainly.

   Q: What favour does the man ask the woman?

Key:

1. B   2. A   3. C   4. D   5. D

Dictation:

   Billy is 14 years old and in the ninth grade. He has a part-time job which gets him up every morning at 5 o'clock. He is a newspaper boy. Each morning, Billy leaves the house at 5:15 to go to the corner, where the newspapers are. The newspapers are delivered to the corner by truck at midnight. He always takes a wagon to carry them.

   In the winter it is still dark when he gets up, but during the rest of the year it is light. Billy must deliver the newspapers to the houses of people on his route in all kinds of weather. He tries to put each paper on the porch where it will be protected from wind and rain or snow. His customers think he does a good job. Sometimes they give him tips.

Chinese Translation (课文参考译文)

钟爱动物

英国人钟爱动物。他们参加动物比赛，捕捉动物，训练动物并喂养动物。他们喜欢从电视新闻节目中收听有关动物的故事，他们还喜欢阅读有关动物的书籍。

很多家庭都养宠物。他们的宠物可以是狗、猫或金鱼，甚或一头猪、一条蛇。一些孤独的老人喜欢他们的猫或狗，就如同喜欢他们的人类朋友一样。当动物爱好者去世时，他们会把钱留给"猫收容所"，"狗收容所"，或者是"老马收容所"。

动物比赛是另一项非常受欢迎的活动。有些被称为"鸽子爱好者"的人参加鸽子比赛。他们在自家的花园或阳台上饲养鸽子并训练它们飞回家。要赛鸽你不必很有钱，但要想赛马情形就不同了。只有那些特别有钱的人才养得起马，并让自己的马参加比赛。在重大赛事上，你能够看见赛马的主人们身着最漂亮的服装，同女王及皇室的其他成员们在一起。实际上，真正去看赛马的人并不多。但是几乎所有的人都能赌马，并且很多人也是这样做的。无论在英国的什么地方，你都能在不远的地方找到一个"赛马赌注登记处"。

照顾和善待动物只是人们喜爱动物的一种表现。捕捉、打猎是英国人的另一大嗜好。例如钓鱼在乡下就是一项最受欢迎的体育运动。数以万计的人喜欢在星期六和星期日静静地坐在湖边或河边等着鱼上钩。另外还有一些人依然热衷于猎狐狸，捕兔子或者射鹿。

英国人为什么如此热衷于动物呢？也许是因为他们与人打交道时过于腼腆和含蓄。"是这样的，"一位老妇人这样说道，"我对我的猫说什么都可以，而它从来不会把我看成是个傻瓜。"

UNIT 9

How to Make Money —And How Not To?

Background Knowledge (背景知识)

1. Peter Minuit（约 1580—1638），彼得·米纽伊特，北美洲新阿姆斯特丹殖民地总督。1626 年初航行到哈得逊河口的荷属殖民地，9 月任荷属美洲新尼德兰省总督。后以少量商品为代价（价值 60 荷盾，相当于 24 美元），从印地安酋长手中购得整个曼哈顿岛。他在该岛南端建立新阿姆斯特丹城，使早期荷兰移民得以在此安家。1664 年曼哈顿岛被英国占领，改名为纽约。

2. 超人（Superman）是个虚构的超级英雄，美国漫画中的经典人物，出现在 DC 漫画公司的同名作品中。其角色还出现在不同的电视剧和电影中。拍过超人的历代电影、电视系列剧有：

电影：

1948 年 *Superman*

1950 年 *Atom Man Vs. Superman*

1951 年 *Superman and the Mole-Men*

1954 年 *Superman Flies Again*

1954 年 *Superman and the Jungle Devil*

1954 年 *Superman in Exile*

1954 年 *Superman in Scotland Yard*

1954 年 *Superman's Peril*

1954 年 *Stamp Day for Superman*

1973 年 *Superman*

1978 年 *Superman*

1980 年 *Superman 2*

1983 年 *Superman 3*

1987 年 *Superman 4: The Quest for Peace*

2006 年 *Superman Returns*

电视系列剧：

1952~1958 年 *Adventures of Superman*

1988~1992 年 *Superboy*

1993~1997 年 *Lois & Clark: The New Adventures of Superman*

2001 年 *Smallville*

Detailed Notes to the Text（课文详解）

1. Others let golden opportunities pass them by.

golden *adj.* 金色的；宝贵的。例如

The child has blue eyes and golden hair.

这个孩子的眼睛是蓝色的，头发是金黄色的。

The whole room was flooded with warm, golden sunlight.

整个房间撒满了温暖的金色阳光。

Good health and peacefulness can make old age the golden years of your life.

好身体和平和的心态能使晚年变成人生中的金色时光。

pass by

1）从旁边经过。例如

A policeman was passing by when the robbery took place.

抢劫发生时，一个警察正好经过。

2）不理，回避。例如

Smith said we passed by him this morning, but we did not see him.

史密斯说今天早上我们从他身边走过而没理他，不过我们真是没看见他。

He passed me by as though he had never in his life seen me before.

他从我身边经过好像他以前从未与我谋面似的。

3）不予理会。例如

I cannot pass the matter by without making a protest.

我不能就这样对此事不提出任何反对意见而一味地保持沉默。

If you try to pass the problems by, they will remain to dog you.

如果你对这些问题不予理睬的话，它们将会一直困扰着你。

2. ..., who bought the island... for 24 dollars' worth of tools and cloth.

worth

1）值多少钱，价值为。例如

It was worth at least fifty francs.

它至少值50法郎。

How much is the picture worth?

这幅画值多少钱？

2）价值与……相当，顶得上。例如

It is worth the price. 它物有所值。

3）值得。例如

They thought the book worth publication.

他们认为此书值得出版。

Is it worth all the trouble?

值得惹这么大的麻烦么？

His suggestion is worth considering.

他的建议值得考虑。

3. **For that price now, you could park your car for a few hours.**

park *vt.* 停车。例如

Where can we park the car?

哪儿可以停车啊？

Don't park the car in the street.

不要把车停在大街上。

4. **Sometimes both sides benefit from a deal.**

benefit *vt.* 对……有利；受益，得到好处（常和 from 连用）。例如

He will benefit from the new way of doing business.

他会从新的经营方式中获利。

deal *n.* 交易，协议（可数名词）。例如

He was trying to make a deal with them.

他试图和他们做笔交易。

News of the deal leaked out.

这笔交易的消息走漏了风声。

5. **Back in the 1920's, a man contacted a company making matches.**

contact *vt.* 和……联系。例如

I will contact my best friend and get his reaction.

我会与我最好的朋友联系，看看他是什么反应。

I shall contact you by telephone on Friday.

周五我会电话与你联系。

6. **He promised that the change would cost them nothing to put into effect, and he only wanted a percentage of the savings they would realize if they went ahead with his idea.**

promise *vt.* 答应；许下承诺。例如

He had promised to see his girl friend home.

他答应送他女朋友回家。

You must promise me to take a thorough rest.

你必须答应彻底休息。

You've got to promise that you won't do that again.

你必须承诺再也不那样做了。

Politicians often promise improvements that will never take place.

政客们经常许诺那些无法实现的改进。

put into effect 使生效；实现。例如

They have already put their plans into effect.

他们的计划已经付诸实施。

When the time is ripe, the scheme will be put into effect.

时机成熟时，计划会被付诸实施的。

saving *n.* 储蓄；存款。例如

It took all our savings to buy the house.

我们花了所有的积蓄买了这所房子。

Many people keep their savings in the National Bank.

很多人都把积蓄存在国家银行。

7. They then spent months trying to find ways to cut costs, ...

cut *vt.* 缩短，削减，减少。例如

We must cut expenses this month.

我们这个月必须削减开销。

We must not cut the cost of education.

我们不应该减少教育支出。

Was your salary cut?

你被减薪了吗？

8. The man was as good as his word.

as good as one's word 说话算话，信守诺言。例如

I am certain that David will do the job on time, because he is as good as his word.

我肯定戴维会按时完成这项工作的，因为他是一个信守诺言的人。

The coach said he would give the players a day off if they won, and he was as good as his word.

教练说如果他们赢了比赛，他将给运动员们放假一天，他说话算话。

9. If you eliminate one of the surfaces, you will have instant savings.

eliminate *vt.* 消除，淘汰。例如

Can the government eliminate poverty?

政府能消除贫困吗？

She went through her essay carefully to eliminate all errors from it.

她把文章从头到尾检查了一遍，把错误都改掉。

instant *adj.* 立即的，迅速的。例如

The telegram asked for an instant reply.

这封电报需要立刻回复。

The sick boy needs instant treatment.

生病的男孩需要立刻接受治疗。

The medicine gives instant relief.

这个药会立刻缓解症状。

10. The company adopted the idea, ...

adopt *vt.* 采取，采纳，采用。例如

Circumstances will force us to adopt this policy.

环境迫使我们接受这项政策。

I adopted their method of making the machine.

我采纳了他们的方法来生产机器。

I liked your idea and adopted it.

我喜欢你的想法并采纳了它。

Key to Exercises（参考答案）

1. 1) Because he bought the island of Manhattan from the local Indians for 24 dollars' worth of tools and cloth. Nowadays 24 dollars wouldn't buy one square foot of office space in New York! For that price now, you could park your car for a few hours.

2) The creators of *Superman* sold their rights of the comic trip hero to a publisher for 65 dollars in 1938 because they were broke. Nowadays the *Superman* movies alone bring in hundreds of millions of dollars!

3) Both the man and the match company.

4) The man thought that his discovery could save the match company a lot of money.

5) He wanted a percentage of the savings.

6) Because they thought if the idea was so obvious to an ordinary person, surely their own research team would have come up with it already.

7) They gave in and called the man in.

8) Yes, he did.

9) The match company presently put two striking surfaces on each match box, but they really only needed one. If they eliminated one of the surfaces, they would have instant savings.

10) Yes, they did.

2.
1) adopt	2) came up with	3) After all
4) drew a blank	5) as good as his word	6) went ahead with
7) passes by	8) worth of	9) alone
10) give in		

3. A.
1) A	2) D	3) A	4) B	5) B
6) C	7) D	8) B	9) C	10) A
11) C	12) A	13) A	14) D	15) B
16) C	17) C	18) B	19) C	20) C
21) B	22) A	23) B	24) C	25) C
26) C	27) A	28) D	29) B	30) C

B.
1) (1) D	(2) B		
2) (1) B	(2) C		
3) (1) B	(2) D	(3) A	(4) C
4) (1) D	(2) A	(3) C	
5) (1) B	(2) C	(3) B	
6) (1) C	(2) D		
7) (1) E	(2) D		
8) (1) D	(2) A		
9) (1) B	(2) D		
10) (1) C	(2) B		

4. A. 1) The man became rich through making wise investment.

2) He blamed himself bitterly for losing the golden opportunity.

3) The procession passed right by my door.

4) A bird in the hand is worth two in the bush.

5) Don't park the car in the street.

6) The business kept losing money and finally went broke.

7) Alone with Nature, you'll never feel lonely.

8) The new hospital will benefit the entire community.

9) The terms are agreeable; it's a deal.

10) We knew she was always as good as her word, so we trusted her.

B. 1) 有些人总让机会擦肩而过。

2) 就拿彼得·米纽伊特来说，他是新阿姆斯特丹（现在的纽约市）的州长，他用价值相当于 24 美元的工具和布匹从当地的印第安人手中买下了曼哈顿岛。

3) 那么，"超人"的首创者的情况又是怎样呢？1938 年，他们因为破产，以 65 美元的价钱把他们的连环画主角的版权卖给了一个出版商。

4) 现在仅《超人》电影一项就能带来数亿美元的收入。

5) 他担保这个变化实施起来不需任何成本。

6) 如果他们实施这个计划的话，他本人只想得到所获节余的一部分。

7) 毕竟，如果这项提议连一个普通人都能想到的话，无疑他们自己的研究小组早就应该会发现了。

8) 他们于是花了数月时间试图找到削减成本的途径，但是没能成功。

9) 这个人言而有信。

10) 如果去掉一个划火面，你们就可以立即节省开支。

5. 1) B   2) A   3) A   4) A   5) B

   6) C   7) D   8) B   9) A   10) D

Reading:

1. 1) C   2) B   3) C   4) B   5) C

2. 1) F   2) T   3) F   4) T   5) T

Listening:

1. M: You can speak English so well. When did you start learning it?

   W: At the age of six.

   Q: When did the woman start learning English?

2. M: How well can you type?

   W: Unfortunately I cannot type very fast.

   Q: Can the woman type very well?

3. M: Hi, dear, are we able to swim this weekend?

   W: Sorry, darling. I am afraid not, because we are going to a concert.

   Q: What are they going to do this weekend?

4. M: I am so surprised that your son can play the guitar so well.

W: He could play the guitar when he was seven.

Q: What can the woman's son play so well?

5. M: We will not be able to play golf tomorrow.

W: Why not?

M: According to the weather forecast, it is raining tomorrow.

Q: Why can't they play golf tomorrow?

Key:

1. A   2. B   3. C   4. D   5. B

Dictation:

Many thousands of years ago, people lived only in hot countries. They did not live in cold countries, because they could not keep warm. Then they learned how to make clothes. When an animal was killed, they cut off its skin. They wrapped the skins around their bodies. The skins kept them warm. Skins, which had fur on them, were the best. Even today some people wear the furs of animals to keep them warm.

At first men did not know how to make fire. Sometimes lightning hit a forest and started a fire. The people took some of this fire to make a fire near their homes. A fire was very important for three reasons. It kept them warm. It frightened away wild animals. They did not attack when they saw a fire. Then another thing was discovered: If you cook food on it, it tastes much better!

Chinese Translation（课文参考译文）

如何赚钱？——如何不赚钱？

有些人看到一项投资时便能判定它是一个有利可图的投资，而有些人却会让绝好的机会擦肩而过。

就拿彼得·米纽伊特来说，他是新阿姆斯特丹（现在的纽约市）的州长，他用价值相当于24美元的工具和布匹从当地的印第安人手中买下了曼哈顿岛。如今的24美元在纽约连1平方英尺的写字间也买不下来！这点儿钱只够你用来停几个小时的车。

《超人》的首创者的情况又是怎样呢？1938年，他们因为破产，以65美元的价钱把他们的连环画主角的版权卖给了一个出版商。现在仅《超人》电影一项就能带来数亿美元的收入。

有时一项交易能够使双方都获益。早在 20 世纪 20 年代，一个人与一家生产火柴的公司联系。他告诉火柴公司他发现如果在他们的生产过程中稍加变化就能为他们节约很多钱。他担保这个变化实施起来不需任何成本。如果他们实施这个计划的话，他本人只想得到所获节余的一部分。

火柴公司对这个人的提议丝毫不感兴趣。如果这项提议连一个普通人都能想到的话，无疑他们自己的研究小组早就应该会发现了。于是他们花了数月时间试图找到削减成本的途径，但是没能成功。他们最后放弃了，再把那个人找了回来。他们同意如果真的能够节约开支的话，他就能够得到他想要的提成。

这个人言而有信。他是这样对他们说的："你们现在的每个火柴盒上有两个用来划火柴的面，但事实上你们只需要一个。如果去掉一个划火面，你们就可以立即节省开支。"

公司采纳了他的建议，节约了开支，并付给了他该得的那份报酬。

你有能够令你成为百万富翁的好主意吗？

UNIT 10

Time to Leave the Nest Yet?

Background Knowledge (背景知识)

　　长期以来，英国的寄宿学校一直是全球家长的首选。通过几个世纪的不断努力，英国的寄宿学校成功地结合传统的价值观和现代的教学手段及设备，高质量的教育使这些学校在英国院校排行榜上名列前茅，几乎所有的学生都可以进入大学深造。在寄宿学校，你不仅可以学到各种知识，了解各国文化和进行体育训练，更可以发掘自身潜力，学会如何充满信心地面对挑战和如何做一个有责任心的公民。

　　在英国共有 2,400 所私立中学，其中 800 余所为寄宿制学校，提供从 7 岁到 18 岁年龄段的教育，包括从小学到中学的课程。一般寄宿学校不会接受 7 岁以下的学生申请，而学生亦需在学校留宿，确保学生参与到寄宿学校提供的运动及社交活动，从而学会独立及适应群体生活。

　　小班授课配之以现代化的教学条件，使每个学生都可以获得更多的个别辅导。学校鼓励学生建立广泛的课外兴趣，这一点深得家长和大学的认可。许多寄宿学校有招收外国学生的传统。

　　寄宿学校分为小学部及中学部，小学部的学生一般为 7 至 13 岁，而中学部则为 13 至 18 岁。大部分的寄宿学校除了根据学生的校内或公开考试来决定学生录取与否，学生亦需通过学校的入学考试。

　　寄宿学校的课程设置适应了英国教育的公共考试体系。这些考试有面向 16 岁学生的 GCSE（普通中等教育证书）或苏格兰教育标准等级证书和面向 18 岁学生的 A-LEVEL（中学高级水平考试）或苏格兰高级证书。同时在许多寄宿学校，学生也可以选择 IB（国际高中毕业考试）课程。现在，越来越多的学校也开设了 GNVQ（全国通用职业资格）课程。

▶ Detailed Notes to the Text （课文详解）

1. Have you ever thought about how ideas about raising children differ from culture to culture?

    differ　*vi.* 不同；持不同意见。例如

    Wisdom differs from cunning.

    聪慧不同于狡猾。

The brothers differ in their interests.

兄弟们的兴趣不同。

He differed with his brother on a political question.

在某个政治问题上他和他的兄弟持不同意见。

2. ... and live in their hometown rather that go away to study elsewhere.

rather than 而不是；与其……不如……。例如

The colour seems green rather than blue.

颜色看起来更应是绿色而不是蓝色。

He ran rather than walked.

与其说他在走不如说他在跑。

Rather than allow the vegetables to go bad, he sold them at half price.

他把蔬菜半价卖掉，而不让它们烂掉。

3. ... and some English parents, apparently desperate to get rid of their children as soon as possible, will consider sending them off to boarding schools as young as eight or nine.

desperate *adj.* 令人绝望的，危急的；迫切的；不顾后果的。例如

He was desperate after the failure of his plans.

他的计划失败后，他绝望了。

He had a desperate desire to justify himself.

他迫切想要澄清自己。

He was desperate for work to provide food for his children.

他迫切想找到一份工作，为的是给孩子们买食物。

4. The parents call it part of growing up; the youngsters call it independence.

grow up 成长；长大。例如

Your children are growing up very quickly.

你的孩子们正在迅速长大。

I grew up on a farm.

我是在农场长大的。

5. Do children benefit from being made independent at an early age, or is it better in the long run for them to stay close to home as long as possible?

in the long run 从长远来说；最后。例如

In the long run, the best is unquestionably the cheapest.

从长远来说，最好的无疑是最便宜的。

Studying may be difficult now, but you will benefit in the long run.

从目前来看学习是艰苦的，但从长远来说你会受益匪浅的。

Key to Exercises（参考答案）

1. 1) The author takes leaving the nest for example.

   2) A French mother will leave her baby at a day-care center before she goes off to her job in the city.

   3) Formal education rarely begins earlier than six.

   4) The majority of people studying at university stay and live in their hometown rather than go away to study elsewhere.

   5) In Britain, primary school starts at five or in some cases four years of age.

   6) Some English parents consider sending their children off as young as eight or nine.

   7) They prefer to go to a university as far away from their hometown as possible.

   8) They live at home with their parents until they marry.

   9) Because he takes pleasure in financing his children.

   10) The father is the head of the family.

2. 1) raise　　　　2) benefit, from　　3) desperate　　　4) In this case

   5) preferable　　6) get rid of　　　7) takes pleasure in　8) bankrolling

   9) tight-knit　　10) In the long run

3. 1) when　　　2) when　　　3) which　　　4) that/which　　5) that

   6) where　　　7) that/which　8) where　　　9) which　　　10) where

   11) where　　12) which　　13) when　　　14) that　　　15) that

   16) that　　　17) that　　　18) which　　　19) that/in which　20) that

   21) that　　　22) that　　　23) whose　　　24) of which　　25) whose

   26) whom　　27) when　　　28) that　　　29) when　　　30) where

4. 1) B　　　2) B　　　3) C　　　4) C　　　5) A

   6) A　　　7) C　　　8) A　　　9) C　　　10) A

   11) D　　12) D　　13) D　　14) A　　15) C

   16) B　　17) B　　18) C　　19) A　　20) D

5. A. 1) What are you thinking about?

2) People's tastes differ.

3) These shoes are comfortable rather than pretty.

4) This old machine is of no use at all now; I shall be glad to get rid of it.

5) What are you going to do when you grow up?

6) He takes great pleasure in doing such things.

7) It pays in the long run to buy goods of high quality.

8) They were desperate for food.

9) I've thought about it for some time.

10) I grew up on a farm.

B. 1) 你有没有想过不同的文化对抚养孩子的看法会有所不同？

2) 法国的母亲在她到城里上班之前会把她 3 岁的孩子送到日托所，尽管正规教育大多是在 6 岁以后才开始。

3) 大多数念大学的人宁愿居住在他们的家乡而不愿到其他的地方去学习。

4) 在英国，小学教育从 5 岁或者有时从 4 岁开始。

5) 有些英国父母，他们显然迫切希望尽早地让孩子们离开他们，于是便在孩子们只有八、九岁的时候就把他们送到寄宿制学校。

6) 到一所尽可能离家远的大学去读书也是多数人所向往的。

7) 在南欧的一些国家，家庭是一个更为亲密、更有凝聚力的集体。

8) 例如在意大利，孩子直到结婚都一直住在父母家里是很正常的。

9) 意大利的父亲甚至还可以继续资助他已成年并已挣工资的儿子，因为作为一家之主，他乐意资助他的孩子们，不管他们有多大。

10) 孩子得益于年幼时就独立呢，还是从长远来看尽可能长地住在家里更好呢？

6. 1) A   2) C   3) C   4) A   5) C

6) A   7) B   8) A   9) C   10) D

7.

Dear Mr. Wilson,

I take great pleasure to introduce my student Li Li to you. Miss Li is studying at our university now, and she is graduating soon. I understand that she is planning to go to your university to pursue her M.A. degree. Miss Li is diligent, resourceful and easy to work with. I am sure that she would become one of the top students. Your help would be greatly appreciated.

Best regards.

Yours sincerely,

Frank Lou

Reading:

1. 1) B   2) A   3) C   4) D   5) B

2. 1) F   2) T   3) F   4) T   5) T

Listening:

1. W: Are you able to repair my computer this Saturday?

   M: Sure.

   Q: Is there anything wrong with the woman's computer?

2. M: I just wonder who can spell that word?

   W: Ask Linda. She knows a lot of words.

   Q: According to the woman, who can spell that word?

3. M: Can you tell me the difference between "be able to" and "can" by giving me an example?

   W: Sure. I can swim but I am not able to swim today because I am busy with my essay.

   M: Thank you.

   Q: What does the man want to know?

4. M: Jim can sing very well.

   W: Really. I know that he can dance well.

   Q: What can Jim do well?

5. M: Will you be able to finish all the readings on time?

   W: I don't think so.

   Q: What cannot the woman do?

Key:

1. B   2. C   3. A   4. C   5. D

Dictation:

    The picture of the United States as a nation of small farmers is no longer true. In former times most of the people in the nation did live on farms, but this has been changing in the past forty years. Now most of the country's population lives in cities.

    However, many people still live in the country and they still play a very important part in American life. They produce most of the food which we eat and which we send abroad to other countries; in addition, other farm crops like cotton and wool are vital to industrial production in the cities.

Chinese Translation （课文参考译文）

父母在，不远游？

你有没有想过不同的文化对抚养孩子的看法会有所不同？就以离家自立为例来说吧。孩子们什么时候才应该步入社会呢？

法国的母亲在她到城里上班之前会把 3 岁的孩子送到日托所，尽管正规教育大多是在 6 岁以后才开始，而且大多数念大学的人宁愿居住在他们的家乡而不愿到其他地方去学习。

在英国，小学教育从 5 岁或者有时从 4 岁开始。有些英国父母，他们显然迫切希望尽早地让孩子们离开他们，于是便在孩子只有八、九岁的时候就把他们送到寄宿制学校。到一所尽可能离家远的大学去读书也是多数人所向往的。父母们称之为成长的一部分；孩子们称之为独立。

在南欧的一些国家，家庭是一个更为亲密、更有凝聚力的集体。例如在意大利，孩子直到结婚都一直住在父母家里是很正常的。意大利的父亲甚至还可以继续资助他已成年并已挣工资的儿子，因为作为一家之主，他乐意资助他的孩子，不管他们有多大。

你是怎么看的？孩子得益于年幼时就独立呢，还是从长远来看尽可能长地住在家里更好呢？

Test One

I. Dialogue Completion (完成对话 5%)

Directions: There are five short incomplete dialogues in this part, each followed by four choices marked A, B, C and D. Choose the best one to complete the dialogue.

1. Tom: Good morning. Can I help you?

   Linda: _____. I want to buy some oranges.

   A. Of course

   B. Yes, please

   C. Why not

   D. Yes

2. Mike: Good morning. What can I do for you?

   Jane: I want to get a sweater for my son.

   Mike: _____. / ?

   A. This way, please

   B. Here you are

   C. Do you like green or white

   D. OK

3. Doctor: Good morning. _____?

   Patient: I have got a headache.

   A. What's the problem

   B. What's the trouble

   C. What's wrong with you

   D. Anything wrong

4. Jim: Are you going to leave school at the end of the term?

   Lisa: Yes. This is my last year at school.

   Jim: What are you going to do then?

   Lisa: I want to find a job. Many jobs are offered in the newspapers.

   Jim: _____?

   Lisa: I want to be a vet.

A. What is interesting

B. What's in your mind

C. Which do you like

D. What do you want

5. Dick: Excuse me, Lucy. Have you got a dictionary?

Lucy: Sorry, I haven't. You may ask Jack.

Dick: _____.

A. Thank you all the same

B. Thank you very much

C. Sorry for the trouble

D. OK, I'll ask Jack

II. Reading Comprehension (阅读理解 20%)

Directions: There are four passages in this part. Each passage is followed by some questions or unfinished statements. For each of them there are four choices marked A, B, C and D. You should decide on the best choice and mark the corresponding letter.

Passage 1

Questions 1 to 5 are based on the following passage:

After inventing dynamite, Swedish-born Alfred Nobel became a very rich man. However, he foresaw its universally destructive powers too late. Nobel preferred not to be remembered as the inventor of dynamite, so in 1895, just two weeks before his death, he created a fund to be used for awarding prizes to people who had made worthwhile contributions to mankind. Originally there were five awards: literature, physics, chemistry, medicine, and peace. Economics was added in 1968, just sixty-seven years after the first awards ceremony.

Nobel's original legacy of nine million dollars was invested, and the interest on this sum is used for the awards, which vary from $30,000 to $125,000.

Every year on December 10, the anniversary of Nobel's death, the awards (gold medal, illuminated diploma and money) are presented to the winners. Sometimes politics plays an important role in the judges' decisions. Americans have won numerous science awards, but relatively few literature prizes.

No awards were presented from 1940 to 1942 at the beginning of World War II. Some people have won two prizes, but this is rare; others have shared their prizes.

1. When did the first award ceremony take place?

   A. In 1895.　　　　B. In 1901.　　　　C. In 1962.　　　　D. In 1968.

2. Why was the Nobel prize established?

   A. To recognize worthwhile contributions to humanity.

   B. To resolve political differences.

   C. To honour the inventor of dynamite.

   D. To spend money.

3. Which of the following statements is NOT true?

   A. Awards vary in monetary value.

   B. Ceremonies are held on December 10 to commemorate Nobel's invention.

   C. Politics can play an important role in selecting the winners.

   D. A few individuals have won two awards.

4. In which area have Americans received the most awards?

   A. Literature.　　　　B. Peace.　　　　C. Economics.　　　　D. Science.

5. In how many fields are prizes awarded?

   A. 2.　　　　B. 5.　　　　C. 6.　　　　D. 10.

Passage 2

Questions 6 to 10 are based on the following passage:

The next great land area that man hopes to colonize is the moon. In size it is nearly equal to the area of North and South America. However, it presents a hostile environment. Temperatures range from +120 to −150 degrees Centigrade. There is no air, no water.

Today there is considerable scientific speculation about living on the moon. When man will begin life on the lunar surface is still not determined. But experts believe that colonization will take place in three steps. First, there will be increasing periods of exploration with temporary shelters. These periods will be followed by longer stays with housing under the surface of the moon and daily necessities brought by the colonizers themselves. Finally, colonies that are self-supporting will be established.

The principal job of the early settlers will be to stay alive. They will have to plant crops under huge domes to produce food and oxygen and find water sources. After this is done, the settlers will have time to explore the possibilities of commercial development and to make discoveries important to science.

The characteristics of the moon that make it bad for human survival may make it ideal for certain kinds of manufacturing. Operations requiring a vacuum, extreme cold, or sterility are examples. Precision ball bearings, industrial diamonds or pharmaceuticals might be produced on the moon.

6. The area of the moon is _____.

   A. about the same as that of North and South America

   B. larger than that of North and South America

   C. equal to that of North and South America

   D. far smaller than that of North and South America

7. The temperature on the moon can be as high as _____.

   A. −150℃   B. +270℃   C. +120℃   D. −30℃

8. According to this passage, the colonization of the moon _____.

   A. will soon be realized

   B. can be done under the lunar surface

   C. is being speculated by many scientists

   D. sounds entirely impossible

9. To stay alive on the moon, the early settlers must first of all be able to _____.

   A. develop commerce

   B. get enough food, oxygen and water

   C. make discoveries important to science

   D. explore the possibilities of industrial development

10. Though the environment on the moon is bad for human survival, it is very good for _____.

    A. making such things as industrial diamonds

    B. all kinds of manufactured goods

    C. medical operations

    D. commercial development

Passage 3

Questions 11 to 15 are based on the following passage:

In Switzerland, six miles west of Geneva, lies a collection of laboratories and buildings, and, most curious of all, a circular mound of earth more than 650 feet in diameter. This cluster has unique importance. It is Europe's one and only atomic city dedicated to investigation of the atom for peaceful purposes.

The strange buildings belong to the European Council for Nuclear Research, more popularly known, from its French initials, as CERN. The council was born when a handful of statesmen and scientific experts met in Paris in 1950. Their aim was "to establish an organization providing for collaboration among European states in nuclear research of a pure scientific and fundamental character."

The CERN agreement was signed in 1953, and work on the atomic city began in 1954. Today CERN's facilities are among the most modern and the most diversified in the world. Impressive as the scientific aspect may be, the real significance of CERN may lie with the thousand people—the scientists, lab workers, and administrative crew drawn from the fourteen member nations—who populate it. British engineers work side by side with Swiss electricians, Yugoslav nuclear physicists, and Dutch mathematicians. The official languages are French and English, with German an unofficial third. But CERN is no tower of Babel—the language of science is universal and all-embracing.

11. The European Council for Nuclear Research was evolved by _____.
    A. the officers of the United Nations
    B. a group of European scientists
    C. the statesmen and scientists of Switzerland
    D. a handful of statesmen and scientific experts

12. CERN was established with the aim of promoting _____.
    A. nuclear research of a fundamental character
    B. collaboration among the world's nuclear scientists
    C. pure study in all fields of science
    D. both A and B

13. CERN's facilities for research are _____.
    A. limited but effective
    B. among the best in the world
    C. rapidly expanding
    D. both A and C

14. The selection says that CERN is not a tower of Babel because _____.
    A. work is the common denominator of all the staff
    B. the language of science is universal

C. CERN has adopted only two official languages

D. all the workers are drawn from one country

15. The real significance of CERN may lie in its staff because they _____.

A. work in international harmony

B. come from all over the world

C. are investigating all phases of human conduct

D. are eliminating the problems of individual nationalism

Passage 4

Questions 16 to 20 are based on the following passage:

Adam Smith, writing in the 1770s, was the first person to see the importance of the division of labour and to explain part of its advantages. He gives as an example of the process by which pins were made in England.

"One man draws out the wire, another strengthens it, a third cuts it, a fourth points it, a fifth grinds it at the top to prepare it to receive the head. To make the head requires two or three distinct operations. To put it on is a separate operation; to polish the pins is another. It is even a trade by itself to put them into the paper. And the important business of making pins is, in this manner, divided into about eighteen distinct operations, which in some factories are all performed by different people, though in others the same man will sometimes perform two or three of them."

Ten men, Smith said, in this way, turned out twelve pounds of pins a day or about 4,800 pins apiece. But if all of them had worked separately and independently without division of labour, they certainly could not, each of them, have made twenty pins in a day and perhaps not even one.

There can be no doubt that division of labour, provided that it is not taken too far, is an efficient way of organising work. Fewer people can make more pins. Adam Smith saw this but he also took it for granted that division of labour is in itself responsible for economic growth and development and that it accounts for the difference between expanding economies and those that stand still. But division of labour adds nothing new; it only enables people to produce more of what they already have.

16. According to the passage, Adam Smith was the first person to _____.

A. take advantage of the division of labour

B. introduce the division of labour into England

C. understand the effects of the division of labour

D. explain the causes of the division of labour

17. Adam Smith saw that the division of labour _____.

A. enabled each worker to make pins more quickly and more cheaply

B. increased the possible output per worker

C. increased the number of people employed in factories

D. improved the quality of pins produced

18. Adam Smith mentioned the number 4,800 in order to _____.

A. show the advantages of the old craft system

B. emphasise how powerful the individual worker was

C. show the advantages of the division of labour

D. emphasise the importance of increased production

19. According to the writer, Adam Smith's mistake was in believing that the division of labour _____.

A. was an efficient way of organising work

B. was an important development in methods of production

C. inevitably led to economic development

D. increased the production of existing goods

20. According to the writer, which of the following is NOT true?

A. Division of labour can enable fewer people to make more pins.

B. Division of labour only helps people to produce more of what they already have.

C. Division of labour is by no means responsible for economic growth.

D. Division of labour is an efficient way of organising work.

III. Vocabulary and Structure (词汇与结构 20%)

Directions: In this part there are 20 incomplete sentences. For each sentence there are four choices marked A, B, C and D. Choose the ONE answer that best completes the sentence.

1. The meeting was put off because we _____ a meeting without John.

   A. are objected to have   B. were objected to having

   C. objected of have   D. objected to having

2. I should have gone to the opera yesterday. It was very good. I wish I _____ yesterday off.

    A. have had
    B. had

    C. have
    D. had had

3. Mary's mother got sick, so she _____.

    A. called on her party
    B. called in her party

    C. called off her party
    D. called out her party

4. Have you seen Henry lately? My mother wants to know _____.

    A. how is he getting along
    B. how he is getting along

    C. what is he getting along
    D. what he is getting along

5. Nancy isn't here. It's my fault. I forgot all about _____ her.

    A. to telephone
    B. to telephone to

    C. telephoning
    D. telephoning to

6. Tom is very diligent. But his pay is not _____ for his work.

    A. enough good
    B. as good enough

    C. good enough
    D. good as enough

7. I cannot come to your dinner tonight. I really would be _____, but I have a date.

    A. glad
    B. glad to have

    C. glad to do it
    D. glad to

8. Weather _____, the picnic will be held as scheduled.

    A. permits
    B. should permit

    C. will permit
    D. permitting

9. How will it turn out? Well, it all _____.

    A. depends
    B. depended

    C. depend on
    D. is depending

10. Officials warned people _____ certain wild fruits.

    A. not to eat
    B. to not eat

    C. not eating
    D. no eating

11. The violin will have to be carefully tuned before it _____.

    A. can be played
    B. is being played

    C. should play
    D. has to play

12. The Bakers arrived last night. If they'd only let us know earlier, _____ at the station.

    A. we'd meet them
    B. we'll meet them

    C. we'd have met them
    D. we'd be meeting them

13. James has just arrived, but I didn't know he _____ until yesterday.

    A. will come

    B. was coming

    C. had been coming

    D. comes

14. I'm disappointed with the new officers elected in our club, but there's no point _____ about it.

    A. to worry

    B. in worrying

    C. with us worrying

    D. if we worry

15. What happens to his machine? It needs _____.

    A. to heat

    B. to be hot

    C. to be hotted

    D. to be heated

16. I left very early last night, but I wish I _____ so early.

    A. didn't leave

    B. haven't left

    C. hadn't left

    D. couldn't leave

17. Take this bag and _____ you can find enough space.

    A. hang it which

    B. hang it there

    C. hang it in which

    D. hang it wherever

18. I have a swimming suit to _____ the cleaners.

    A. being sent to

    B. send to

    C. be sent to

    D. be sending to

19. The reason I plan to go is _____ if I don't.

    A. because she will be disappointed

    B. that she will be disappointed

    C. because she will have a disappointment

    D. on account she will be disappointed

20. If you _____ that late movie last night, you wouldn't be sleepy.

    A. haven't watched

    B. hadn't watched

    C. didn't watch

    D. wouldn't watch

IV. Cloze Test (完形填空 20%)

Directions: There are 20 blanks in the following passage, and for each blank there are four choices marked A, B, C and D at the end of the passage. You should choose the ONE answer that best fits into the passage.

I can clearly remember the first time I __1__ Mr. Andrews, my old headmaster, __2__ it's over twenty years ago. During the war I had been at school __3__ the north of England, but my family had just returned to London. There were not enough schools left for children __4__ and my father had to go from __5__, asking them to take me __6__ pupil. I used to go with him but he had __7__ hard time trying to persuade people even to see him that I seldom had to do __8__. We had been __9__ all the schools near __10__ we lived, but the more my father argued, the more impossible it became. In the end, we went to a school about five miles __11__ home. The headmaster kept us __12__ at least an hour. While we were waiting, I looked round at the school building __13__ was one of those old Victorian structures, completely __14__ but still standing. I could hear the boys playing in the playground outside. When the headmaster's secretary finally let us __15__ his office, Mr. Andrews spoke to me first. "Why do you want to come here?" he said. I had been thinking __16__ something about studying but I couldn't help __17__ the boys outside. "I don't know __18__ in London," I said. "I'd like to play with the other boys. I read a lot of books, too," I added. "All right," Mr. Andrews said. "We have one place free, __19__."

My two years at that school were among the __20__ of my life.

1. A. found   B. met   C. began knowing   D. knew

2. A. although   B. even if   C. in spite   D. as if

3. A. on   B. at   C. over   D. in

4. A. to go   B. go   C. to go to   D. go to

5. A. one to other   B. each to other   C. one to the next   D. one to another

6. A. as a   B. as   C. like   D. like a

7. A. so   B. a so   C. such a   D. such

8. A. no test   B. any tests   C. one test   D. some tests

9. A. to   B. in   C. for   D. at

10. A. which   B. where   C. the place that   D. that

11. A. to   B. from   C. away from   D. around

12. A. wait for   B. to wait   C. to wait for   D. waiting for

13. A. which   B. what   C. it   D. one of which

14. A. to date   B. up to date   C. over the date   D. out of date

15. A. in   B. into   C. to   D. from

16. A. of saying   B. about telling   C. to say   D. to tell

17. A. remember   B. to remember   C. remembering   D. remembered

18. A. none   B. anyone   C. no one   D. someone

19. A. in fact   B. as a fact   C. in the fact   D. for the fact

20. A. happier   B. happiest   C. more happy   D. happy

V. Mistake Identification (挑错练习 10%)

Directions: Each of the following sentences has four underlined parts marked A, B, C and D. Identify the one that is NOT correct.

1. He suffers <u>from</u> Aids, <u>which</u> <u>are</u> <u>a kind of</u> infectious disease.
            A   B C   D

2. <u>Nowadays</u> <u>athletics</u> <u>have</u> been promoted <u>at</u> the institute.
     A   B   C   D

3. He arrived <u>at</u> the hotel, but his <u>baggages</u> <u>was</u> still <u>on</u> the way.
           A   B   C   D

4. The <u>news</u> <u>are</u> going <u>to be</u> <u>heard</u> everywhere.
     A B   C   D

5. Riding on the swings and <u>playing</u> with the ducks in the pond <u>was</u> our children's <u>greatest</u>
                         A   B   C

   pleasure when we took <u>them</u> to the park.
                        D

6. If you <u>spare</u> no <u>effort</u> in working, <u>one</u> will succeed <u>without</u> doubt.
         A   B   C   D

7. <u>In the past</u>, the rulers of the country <u>has been</u> selfish, but the <u>present</u> king has great
    A   B   C

   respect and concern <u>for</u> his people.
                  D

8. <u>What happened</u> in New York <u>were</u> a reaction from city workers, <u>including</u> firemen and
   A   B   C

   policemen who had been laid off from <u>their</u> jobs.
                           D

9. Every doctor <u>must know</u> both medical theory and technique <u>so that</u> he can apply <u>it</u> in
              A   B   C

   <u>helping</u> his patients.
   D

10. The government <u>has</u> discussed the matter <u>for a long time</u> but <u>they</u> have shown no <u>signs</u>
               A   B   C   D

   of reaching an agreement.

VI. Translation (翻译 20%)

1. Translate the following sentences into English (汉译英):

1) 上周在礼品店，艾米莉遇见了一位著名歌星。

2) 上次学校旅行时蒂娜和她的朋友们住在一块儿。

3) 我们班被分成了三个组。

4) 他们以前放学后总是打篮球。

5) 她酷爱言情小说。

2. Translate the following sentences into Chinese (英译汉):

1) Education is not an end, but a means to an end.

2) In other words, we do not educate children only for the aim of educating them.

3) Our purpose is to fit them for life.

4) Life is varied; so is education.

5) As soon as we realize this fact, we will understand that it is very important to choose a proper system of education.

VII. Writing (写作 5%)

Directions: You are required to write a notice according to the following instructions given in Chinese.

说明：请你以学院办公室的名义于 2007 年 4 月 11 日写一份通知。通知全体教授和副教授于下周一（4 月 18 日）下午两点在学院会议室开会，讨论国际学术交流问题，请大家准时出席。

Test Two

I. Dialogue Completion (完成对话 5%)

Directions: There are five short incomplete dialogues in this part, each followed by four choices marked A, B, C and D. Choose the best one to complete the dialogue.

1. Chris: It is Independence Day today.

   Nick: _____?

   Chris: Americans. They celebrate the birth of their motherland.

   A. Whose holiday is it

   B. Who celebrate it

   C. Which country's holiday is it

   D. What is it

2. Charley: Come on, Steve. _____.

   Steve: Wait a moment. I just have to close up the shop.

   Charley: OK.

   A. You are always so slow

   B. Hurry up

   C. What are you doing?

   D. It's time to go

3. Mike: Good afternoon. _____?

   Jack: Yes, please. I'd like to buy a camera.

   A. What do you want to buy

   B. What do you like

   C. Anything you want to buy

   D. Can I help you

4. Simon: Is there anything I can do for you?

   George: Yes, please. Could you tell me when the bus leaves?

   Simon: I'm afraid you've just missed it.

   George: _____?

   Simon: In ten minutes.

   George: Thank you very much.

A. How about the next one

B. Do you know the next one

C. How often does the bus run

D. How far is the next one

5.   Rosie: Sorry, I overslept. My clock didn't go off this morning.

Francie: _____?

Rosie: That's right, even though I did set the alarm last night.

Francie: Your clock never works. Perhaps you should buy a new one.

A. Really

B. How come

C. Again

D. Why

II. Reading Comprehension (阅读理解 20%)

Directions: There are four passages in this part. Each passage is followed by some questions or unfinished statements. For each of them there are four choices marked A, B, C and D. You should decide on the best choice and mark the corresponding letter.

Passage 1

Questions 1 to 5 are based on the following passage:

Ever since humans have inhabited the earth, they have made use of various forms of communication. Generally, this expression of thoughts and feelings has been in the form of oral speech. When there is a language barrier, communication is accomplished through sign language in which motions stand for letters, words, and ideas. Tourists, the deaf and the mute, have had to resort to this form of expression. Many of these symbols of whole words are very picturesque and exact and can be used internationally; spelling, however, cannot.

Body language transmits ideas or thoughts by certain actions, either intentionally or unintentionally. A wink can be a way of flirting or indicating that the party is only joking. A nod signifies approval, while shaking the head indicates a negative reaction.

Other forms of nonlinguistic language can be found in Braille (a system of raised dots read with the fingertips), signal flags, Morse code, and smoke signals. Road maps and picture signs also guide, warn, and instruct people.

While verbalization is the most common form of language, other systems and techniques also express human thoughts and feelings.

1. Which of the following best summarizes this passage?

 A. When language is a barrier, people will find other forms of communication.

 B. Everybody uses only one form of communication.

 C. Nonlinguistic language is invaluable to foreigners.

 D. Although other forms of communication exist, verbalization is the fastest.

2. Which of the following statements is NOT true?

 A. There are many forms of communication in existence today.

 B. Verbalization is the most common form of communication.

 C. The deaf and the mute use an oral form of communication.

 D. Ideas and thoughts can be transmitted by body language.

3. Which form other than oral speech would be most commonly used among blind people?

 A. Picture signs.　　　 B. Braille.　　　 C. Body language.　　　 D. Signal flags.

4. How many different forms of communication are mentioned here?

 A. 5.　　　 B. 7.　　　 C. 9.　　　 D. 11.

5. Sign language is said to be very picturesque and exact and can be used internationally except for _____ .

 A. spelling　　　 B. ideas　　　 C. whole words　　　 D. expressions

Passage 2

Questions 6 to 10 are based on the following passage:

　　Time spent in a bookshop can be most enjoyable, whether you are a book-lover or merely there to buy a book as a present. You may even have entered the shop just to find shelter from a sudden shower. Whatever the reason, you can soon become totally unaware of your surroundings, you soon become engrossed in some book or other, and usually it is only much later that you realize you have spent too much time there and must dash off to keep some forgotten appointment.

　　This opportunity to escape the realities of everyday life is the main attraction of a bookshop. A bookshop is very much like a music shop. You can wander round such places to your heart's content. It is a good shop; no assistant will approach you with the evitable greeting, "Can I help you?" You needn't buy anything you don't want. In a bookshop an assistant should remain in the background until you have finished browsing. Then, and only then, are his services necessary.

Once a medical student had to read a textbook, which was far too expensive for him to buy. He couldn't obtain it from the library and the only copy he could find was in a certain bookshop. Every afternoon, therefore, he would go along to the shop and read a little of the book at a time. One day, however, he was disappointed to find the book missing from its usual place. He was about to leave, when he noticed the owner of the shop beckoning to him. Expecting to be told off, he went towards him. To his surprise, the owner pointed to the book which was tucked away in a corner. "I put it there in case anyone was tempted to buy it!" he said, and left the delighted student to continue his reading.

6. You may spend a long time in a bookshop because _____.

    A. the books are very attractive

    B. you start reading one of the books

    C. it is raining outside

    D. you have to make sure you don't buy a dull book as a present

7. In a good bookshop _____.

    A. nobody takes any notice of you

    B. the assistant greets you in a friendly way

    C. your heart is contented

    D. you feel that you are in a music shop

8. The medical student went to the bookshop every day _____.

    A. to see if the book he wanted was in its usual place

    B. to read the book without buying it

    C. to talk with the shop owner

    D. to try to get the textbook

9. The textbook the medical student was interested in was tucked away in a corner _____.

    A. to prevent anyone from buying it

    B. because the medical student might take it away

    C. in case the medical student was tempted to buy it

    D. because the medical student was tempted to buy it

10. The medical student was surprised because _____.

    A. he saw the owner beckoning to him

    B. the book wasn't in its usual place

    C. he had expected the owner to be angry with him

    D. he was about to leave

Passage 3

Questions 11 to 15 are based on the following passage:

Do you find getting up in the morning so difficult that it is painful? This might be called laziness, but Dr. Kleitman has a new explanation. He has proved that everyone has a daily energy cycle.

During the hours when you labour through your work you may say that you are "hot". That is true. The time of day when you feel most energetic is when your cycle of body temperature is at its peak. For some people the peak comes during the forenoon. For others it comes in the afternoon or evening. No one has discovered why this is so, but it leads to such familiar monologues as: "Get up, John! You'll be late for work again!" The possible explanation to the trouble is that John is at his temperature-and-energy peak in the evening. Much family quarrelling ends when husbands and wives realize what these energy cycles mean, and which cycle each member of the family has.

You can't change your energy cycle, but you can learn to make your life fit it better. Habit can help, Dr. Kleitman believes. Maybe you're sleepy in the evening but feel you must stay up later anyway. Counteract your cycle to some extent by habitually staying up later than you want to. If your energy is low in the morning but you have an important job to do early in the day, rise before your usual hour. This won't change your cycle, but you'll get up steam and work better at your low point.

Get off to a slow start, which saves your energy. Get up with a leisurely yawn and stretch. Sit on the edge of the bed a minute before putting your feet on the floor. Avoid the troublesome search for clean clothes by laying them out the night before. Whenever possible, do routine work in the afternoon and save tasks requiring more energy or concentration for your sharper hours.

11. If a person finds getting up early a problem, most probably _____.
    A. he is a lazy person
    B. he refuses to follow his own energy cycle
    C. he is not sure when his energy is low
    D. he is at his peak in the afternoon or evening

12. Which of the following may lead to family quarrels according to the passage?
    A. Unawareness of energy cycles.
    B. Familiar monologues.
    C. A change in a family member's energy cycle.
    D. Attempts to control the energy cycle of other family members.

13. If one wants to work more efficiently at his low point in the morning, he should _____.

    A. change his energy cycle   B. overcome his laziness

    C. get up earlier than usual   D. go to bed earlier

14. You are advised to rise with a yawn and stretch because it will _____.

    A. help to keep your energy for the day's work

    B. help you to control your temper early in the day

    C. enable you to concentrate on your routine work

    D. keep your energy cycle under control all day

15. Which of the following statements is NOT true?

    A. Getting off to work with a minimum effort helps save one's energy.

    B. Dr. Kleitman explains why people reach their peaks at different hours of day.

    C. Habit helps one adapt to his own energy cycle.

    D. Children have energy cycles, too.

Passage 4

Questions 16 to 20 are based on the following passage:

In November 1965, New York was blacked out by an electricity failure. The authorities promised that it would not happen again. Pessimists were certain that it would occur again within five years at the latest. In July 1977, there was a repeat performance, which produced varying degrees of chaos throughout the city of eight million people. In 1965, the failure occurred in the cool autumn and at a time of comparative prosperity. In 1977, the disaster was much more serious because it came when unemployment was high and the city was suffering from one of its worst heat waves.

In 1965, there was little crime or looting during the darkness, and fewer than a hundred people were arrested. In 1977, hundreds of stores were broken into and looted. Looters smashed shop windows and helped themselves to jewelry, clothes or television sets. Nearly 4,000 people were arrested but far more disappeared into the darkness of the night. The number of policemen available was quite inadequate and they wisely refrained from using their guns against mobs, which far out-numbered them and included armed men.

Hospitals had to treat hundreds of people cut by glass from shop windows. Banks and most businesses remained closed the next day. The blackout started at 9:30 p.m. when lightning hit and knocked out vital cables. Many stores were thus caught by surprise.

The vast majority of New Yorkers, however, were not involved in looting. They helped strangers, distributed candles, and batteries, and tried to survive in a nightmare world without traffic lights, refrigerators, water and electric power. For twenty-four hours, New York realized how helpless it was without electricity.

16. Look at the first paragraph. Who were right, the authorities or the pessimists?

A. The authorities.   B. The pessimists.

C. Both.   D. Neither.

17. In what way was the blackout of 1977 not really a repeat performance?

A. There was much more disorder.

B. This time the electricity supply failed.

C. It was quite unexpected.

D. It did not occur within five years of 1965.

18. As far as maintaining the peace was concerned, conditions in 1977 were comparatively

_____.

A. more favorable   B. less favorable

C. unchanged   D. improved

19. What caused the blackout in July 1977?

A. Excessive heat probably made people switch on too many electrical appliances.

B. Because of unemployment, some machines were not in proper working order.

C. During a storm, lightning damaged supply cables.

D. The passage does not mention the cause.

20. Why did many looters manage to escape?

A. The police could not see them in the dark.

B. Many of the looters were armed with guns.

C. There were not enough policemen to catch them all.

D. They were hidden inside big buildings.

III. Vocabulary and Structure (词汇与结构 20%)

Directions: In this part there are 20 incomplete sentences. For each sentence there are four choices marked A, B, C and D. Choose the ONE answer that best completes the sentence.

1. I think he has _____ in that sort of work.

A. much experiences   B. some experience

C. little experiences   D. many experiences

2. The number of accidents on roads _____.

    A. has increased   B. were increased

    C. are increased   D. have increased

3. We need a chairman _____.

    A. whom everyone has confidence   B. in whom everyone has confidence

    C. whom everyone have confidence   D. who everyone has confidence

4. _____ and you'll see a high building.

    A. Turning to the left   B. To turn the left

    C. Turn to the left   D. To the left

5. She is _____ something stupid.

    A. so clever for doing   B. too clever to do

    C. very clever as to do   D. clever enough to do

6. _____ his parents sent him to school.

    A. Being seven years old   B. When at seven

    C. When he was seven years old   D. When seven years old

7. _____, you have to study.

    A. Whether you like it or not   B. However you like it

    C. Unless you like it   D. No matter you like it

8. _____, the retired worker is still working hard for the people.

    A. Old as he is   B. Though old he is

    C. However he is old   D. Unless he is old

9. _____, the pupil raised his hand.

    A. Not understand the question   B. Having not understood the question

    C. Not having understood the question   D. Not being understood of the question

10. Writing stories _____ what I enjoy most.

    A. are   B. is

    C. were   D. have been

11. You, who _____ ready to offer him assistance, are a true friend of his.

    A. are   B. is

    C. was   D. has been

12. I haven't seen you for quite some time. What _____ lately?

    A. did you do   B. were you doing

    C. have you been doing   D. had you been doing

13. Clark never used to smoke, _____?

    A. did he   B. usedn't he

    C. didn't he   D. was he

14. I am the only person who is to blame, _____?

    A. am I   B. aren't I

    C. isn't I   D. am not I

15. Never in his life _____.

    A. Frank has done anything more careless

    B. Frank has done more careless anything

    C. has Frank done anything more careless

    D. has anything been done more careless

16. We weren't happy about the reward. _____.

    A. Neither wasn't Eileen   B. So wasn't Eileen

    C. Not wasn't Eileen   D. Neither was Eileen

17. By the next September, Bruce _____ here for five years.

    A. has been studying   B. will be studying

    C. will have been studying   D. will have been studied

18. I didn't hear him. Please repeat _____.

    A. what he said   B. what was he saying

    C. what did he say   D. what had he said

19. There are pictures of _____.

    A. men fighting   B. men are fighting

    C. that man are fighting   D. men fight

20. The new instrument doesn't need _____ yet.

    A. to be clean   B. cleaning

    C. being cleaned   D. having been cleaned

IV. Cloze Test (完形填空 20%)

Directions: There are 20 blanks in the following passage, and for each blank there are four choices marked A, B, C and D at the end of the passage. You should choose the ONE answer that best fits into the passage.

Yesterday was __1__. He got a lot of presents __2__ his friends and family. All the gifts were wrapped __3__ coloured paper. __4__ of __5__ __6__ large, but others were very small. Some __7__ heavy, and others were light. One square package was blue; there was a book in it. Another one was long and narrow; it had an umbrella in it. Jim's sister gave him a big, __8__ package. He thought it __9__ a ball, but it __10__. When he __11__ the yellow paper that covered it, he saw that it was a globe of the world.

After that his brother gave him __12__ gift. It was a big box __13__ green paper. Jim opened it and found another box __14__ red paper. He removed the paper and saw a third box; this one was blue in colour.

Everyone laughed __15__ Jim opened the boxes. There were six of them! In the last one he found a small white envelope. There was a piece of paper in the envelope which __16__ : "Go to the big bedroom. Look __17__ the closet near the high window. You will see three suitcases: a black one, a brown one and a gray one. Your birthday present is in one of these."

Jim __18__ the large bedroom. He went to the closet and began __19__ the suitcases. He had to open all of them __20__ he saw his brother's present. He was very happy. It was just what Jim wanted—a portable typewriter.

1. A. birthday of Jim   B. Jim birthday   C. Jim's birthday   D. Jim-birth-day

2. A. at   B. away with   C. back from   D. from

3. A. in   B. by   C. with   D. of

4. A. Most   B. Many   C. Some   D. Much

5. A. the packages   B. packages   C. the package   D. package

6. A. is   B. are   C. was   D. were

7. A. was   B. were   C. had been   D. have been

8. A. circle   B. around   C. round   D. ring

9. A. had been   B. was   C. were   D. would be

10. A. hadn't been   B. would not be   C. weren't   D. was not

11. A. removed   B. took out   C. took off   D. took away

12. A. the other   B. other   C. an other   D. another

13. A. covering with   B. enveloping   C. wrapped in   D. wrapped by

14. A. wrapping in   B. covering in   C. covered with   D. enveloping in

15. A. while   B. before   C. as soon as   D. as

16. A. said   B. wrote   C. reads   D. speaks

17. A. at   B. in   C. for   D. around

18. A. went to   B. came out   C. went in   D. came to

19. A. open   B. opening   C. close   D. closing

20. A. unless   B. after   C. until   D. before

V. Mistake Identification (挑错练习 10%)

Directions: Each of the following sentences has four underlined parts marked A, B, C and D. Identify the one that is NOT correct.

1. He <u>fell</u> asleep immediately <u>last</u> night; he must <u>be</u> very tired.
         A B   C   D

2. I shall never <u>forget</u> <u>to meet</u> Premier Zhou <u>during</u> his inspection <u>of</u> our factory.
                  A   B   C   D

3. I <u>wonder</u> if he could get it <u>have done</u> <u>before</u> tomorrow.
     A B   C   D

4. We were busy <u>to get</u> things ready <u>for</u> the trial production <u>when</u> he phoned <u>us</u>.
                 A   B   C   D

5. <u>To fail</u> several times, they <u>really</u> <u>need</u> <u>some</u> encouragement now.
     A   B C D

6. <u>I have been studying</u> here <u>for</u> four years, by <u>next</u> summer I shall <u>be graduated</u>.
           A   B   C   D

7. <u>To succeed</u> in <u>a</u> scientific research project <u>one</u> needs <u>be</u> a persistent person.
       A   B   C   D

8. <u>After</u> the traffic accident he <u>laid</u> in <u>bed</u> for two weeks, waiting for his wound <u>to heal</u>.
     A   B C   D

9. <u>A</u> big chemical fertilizer plant <u>is</u> built <u>in</u> the suburbs <u>of</u> city now.
   A   B C   D

10. The man <u>rose</u> <u>from</u> the ground, <u>beaten</u> the dust <u>off</u> his clothes.
           A B   C   D

VI. Translation (翻译 20%)

1. Translate the following sentences into English (汉译英):

1) 男孩子们用了一上午的时间探讨这个问题的答案。

2) 人是唯一能说话的动物。

3) 世界上没有哪种动物可以每天都不睡觉。

4) 通过考试的最好方法是每天努力学习。

5) 走时别忘记锁门。

2. Translate the following sentences into Chinese (英译汉):

1) When children learn a language, they learn grammar as well as vocabulary.

2) He was, in fact, one of the most successful writers of his time in his country.

3) You cannot expect her to be on time if you are late yourself.

4) My friend and I would like to go to the concert, but neither of us has got a ticket.

5) The railroad was very important in encouraging westward movement.

VII. Writing (写作 5%)

Directions: You are required to write a telephone message in no less than 60 words according to the following instructions given in Chinese.

说明：按电话留言的格式和要求，以秘书 Helena 的名义，给 Mr. White 写一份电话留言，包括以下内容：

1. 来电人：Honeywell 公司的 Mr. Johnson；

2. 来电时间：2007 年 2 月 25 日上午 10 时；

3. 事由：Mr. Johnson 明天要出差去北京，月底才回来，因此只好取消原定与 Mr. White 2 月 30 日上午的约会，等出差回来后再与 Mr. White 约时间会面。

Test Three

I. Dialogue Completion (完成对话 5%)

Directions: There are five short incomplete dialogues in this part, each followed by four choices marked A, B, C and D. Choose the best one to complete the dialogue.

1. Adriana: I heard you're moving to New York.

   Ryan: Yes. I've got an offer in upstate New York.

   Adriana: _____.

   Ryan: Me, too. Let's keep in touch.

   A. Oh, that's great! But I'm going to miss you.

   B. Oh, I'm sorry to hear that because I'm going to miss you.

   C. Really? Are you going to miss me?

   D. That's too bad. I'm going to miss you.

2. Rex: Hi, Burt. I heard you're looking for a new job.

   Burt: Yeah. I just had an interview yesterday.

   Rex: Oh. _____?

   Burt: I think I did well. They said they would make a decision by this Friday.

   A. Did you do well

   B. How do you find it

   C. How was everything going

   D. How did it go

3. Cashier: How can I help you?

   Jackie: Could you break a 20 for me?

   Cashier: _____?

   Jackie: Could I have two fives and the rest in ones?

   A. Why not. How do you want it

   B. Of course. What do you want

   C. Sure. How do you want it

   D. Sure. How shall I break it

4. Michael: I was locked out of my apartment last night.

   Joan: Then how did you get in?

Michael: I climbed in from the window.

Joan: _____? Oh, my! You're brave.

Michael: Thank you. In fact, I didn't realize that I was such a good climber.

A. You what

B. Could you say it again, please

C. Are you kidding

D. How dare

5. Tom: Can you do me a favor?

Jamie: Sure. _____?

Tom: Can you keep an eye on my bag, please? Nature's calling.

Jamie: Sure. Will you be long?

Tom: No, I just want to use the bathroom.

Jamie: Go ahead. It'll be safe with me.

A. What

B. What can I do for you

C. How can I help you

D. What is it

II. Reading Comprehension (阅读理解 20%)

Directions: There are four passages in this part. Each passage is followed by some questions or unfinished statements. For each of them there are four choices marked A, B, C and D. You should decide on the best choice and mark the corresponding letter.

Passage 1

Questions 1 to 5 are based on the following passage:

You have been badly injured in a car accident. It is necessary to give you a blood transfusion because you lost a great deal of blood in the accident. However special care must be taken in selecting new blood for you. If the blood is too different from your own, the transfusion could kill you.

There are four basic types of blood: A, B, AB and O. A simple test can indicate a person's blood type. Everybody is born with one of these four types of blood. Blood type, like hair colour and height, is inherited from parents.

Because of substances contained in each type, the four groups must be transfused carefully. Basically, A and B cannot be mixed. A and B cannot receive AB, but AB may receive A or B. O can give to any other group; *hence*, it is often called the universal donor. For the opposite reason, AB sometimes called the universal recipient. However, because so many reactions can occur in transfusions, patients usually receive only salt or plasma (liquid) until their blood can be matched as exactly as possible in the blood bank of a hospital. In this way, it is possible to avoid any bad reactions to the transfusion.

There is a relationship between your blood type and your nationality. Among Europeans and people of European ancestry, about 42 percent have type A while 45 percent have type O. The rarest is type AB. Other races have different percentages. For example, some American Indian groups have nearly 100 percent type O.

1. A good title for this selection is _____.

   A. Getting Blood and Plasma   B. Special Blood and Colors

   C. Human Blood Types   D. The Blood Bank of a Hospital

2. The word "hence" in line 10 means _____.

   A. always   B. often   C. therefore   D. seldom

3. The author suggests that the third most common blood type of Europeans is _____.

   A. A   B. B   C. AB   D. O

4. People with type A blood can receive _____.

   A. AB   B. B   C. O   D. None of the above

5. If you need a transfusion, the best and safest blood for you is _____.

   A. type AB   B. exactly the same type as yours

   C. a mixture of salt, plasma, and type O   D. type A

Passage 2

Questions 6 to 10 are based on the following passage:

Not long ago, the only time you'd see a robot is when you were reading a novel or watching a movie such as *Star Wars*. Today, however, science stories are fast becoming science facts. Robots are starting to make their presences felt in our everyday lives.

These robots come in all sizes, shapes, and colors. They all have the same type of man-made "brain". Leading the robot revolution are industrial robots—robots that work in factories. Industrial robots perform different kinds of jobs that are often boring and sometimes dangerous. Robots are also coming to American homes, though not as quickly as they are entering factories. These robots aren't as friendly and bright as those you saw in *Star Wars*. But, their makers say, today's home robots "walk", sense objects in their way (and sometimes knock into them), and even carry objects (which they sometimes drop). Well, nobody's perfect.

We may laugh at home robots today, but some day they may see and hear better than humans do. We humans can only see certain wavelengths of light, and hear certain sounds. That's because the abilities of our eyes and ears are limited. Robots, however, need not have the same limits as we have. Robots may also be equipped with devices that pick up information humans can't.

To understand what their sensing devices pick up is a hard job. Remember, man-made brains handle information, including all kinds of data, as zeroes and ones. Imagine the difficulty in trying to explain to a robot what a football looks like—using only zeroes and ones.

6. From the passage, we can see that factory robots _____ .

    A. help to improve other types of robots

    B. are most active in industrial revolution

    C. are playing a more important role than other types of robots

    D. are the tallest type among robots

7. It seems that home robots are _____ .

    A. more widely used than factory robots

    B. less common than factory robots

    C. capable of doing any kind of housework

    D. free from making mistakes while performing duties

8. Robots may deal with information that humans can't. Which of the following is NOT one of the reasons?

    A. They do not have so many limits as humans do.

    B. They have man-made brains.

    C. They may be equipped with a special kind of sensing device.

    D. They handle information by using zeroes and ones.

9. The development of robots suggests that _____ .

    A. science and technology are developing rapidly

    B. people are interested in new inventions

C. machines are more capable than humans

D. robots can be very interesting

10. According to this passage, present home robots are _____.

A. better than humans in seeing and hearing

B. as capable as those in *Star Wars*

C. can pick up objects more quickly than humans

D. sometimes perform wrong actions

Passage 3

Questions 11 to 14 are based on the following passage:

Crime has its own cycles, a magazine reported some years ago. Police records that were studied for five years from over 2,400 cities and towns show a surprising link between changes in the season and crime patterns. The pattern of crime has varied very little over a long period of years. Murder reaches its high during July and August, as do other violent attacks. Murder, moreover, is more than seasonal: it is a weekend crime. It is also a nighttime crime: 62 percent of murders are committed between 6 p.m. and 6 a.m.

Unlike the summer high in crimes of bodily harm, robbing has a different cycle. You are most likely to be robbed between 6 p.m. and 2 a.m. on a Saturday night in December, January, or February. The month with least crimes of all is May—except for one strange fact. More dog bites are reported in this month than in any other month of the year.

Apparently our seasonal cycles of knowledge are completely different from our tendencies for crimes. Professor Huntington made extensive studies to discover the seasons when people read serious books, attend scientific meetings and get highest results on examinations. In all cases, he found a spring high and autumn high separated by a summer low.

Possibly, high temperature and high humidity cause our strange and violent summer actions, but police officials are not sure. "There is, of course, no proof of a connection between humidity and murder," they say. "Why murder's high time should come in the summer time we really don't know."

11. A good title of the passage would be _____.

A. Crime Cycles

B. Summer Crimes

C. A Time for Murder

D. The Most Peaceful Month

12. According to the passage, _____.

A. there is a link between changes in the seasons and crime patterns

B. crime is not linked to the cycle of the weekdays

C. there is a sure connection between murder and hot weather

D. there is a connection between robbing and murder

13. A murder would most likely occur _____.

A. on a weekend night in summer

B. on a weekend afternoon in summer

C. on a weekend night in winter

D. on a weekday afternoon in spring

14. Which of the following statements is most likely to be true?

A. There is proof of a connection between humidity and murder.

B. Murder's high time never comes in the summer time.

C. High temperature and high humidity surely cause our strange and violent summer actions.

D. The reasons for the violent actions and the murder's high time are still unknown.

Passage 4

Questions 15 to 20 are based on the following passage:

In the US, people prefer waiting for a table to sitting with people they don't know. This means a hostess may not seat a small group until a small table is available, even if a large one is. If you are sitting at a table with people you don't know, it is impolite to light up a cigarette without first asking if it will disturb them.

At American restaurants and coffee shops you are usually served tap water before you order. You may find the bread and butter is free, and if you order coffee, you may get a free refill.

Most cities and towns have no rules about opening and closing times for stores or restaurants, though they usually do make rules for bars. Especially in large cities, stores may be open 24 hours a day.

Servings in restaurants are often large, too large for many people. If you can't finish your meal but would like to enjoy the food later, ask your waitress or waiter for a "doggie bag". It may have a picture of a dog on it, but everybody knows you're taking the food for yourself.

Supper and dinner are both words for the evening meal. Some people have "Sunday dinner". This is an especially big noon meal.

Tips are not usually added to the check. They are not included in the price of the meal, either. A tip of about 15% is expected and you should leave it on the table when you leave. In some restaurants, a check is brought on a plate and you put your money there. Then the waiter or waitress brings you your change.

15. Which of the following statements is true?

   A. American people like sitting with people they don't know.

   B. Hostess always seats a small group at a large table.

   C. American people never sit with people they don't know.

   D. American people would not light a cigarette if the people who sit at the same table mind their smoking.

16. What is served before you order?

   A. Bread.   B. Butter.   C. Coffee.   D. Cold water.

17. What do American people always do when servings are too large for them?

   A. They take the food home with a doggie bag for their dogs.

   B. They leave the food on the table and go away.

   C. They take the food home with a doggie bag and enjoy the food later.

   D. They ask the waitress or waiter to keep the food for them.

18. Sunday dinner is _____.

   A. a dinner in the evening   B. a big noon meal

   C. a big supper on Sunday   D. a supper on Sunday

19. This selection takes the form of _____.

   A. a novel   B. an introduction

   C. a diary entry   D. a business letter

20. Which statement is NOT mentioned in the passage?

   A. Tips are not usually included in the total check.

   B. A 15 percent tip in large cities indicates satisfactory service.

   C. People tip waiters and waitresses.

   D. People always put tips on the table.

III. Vocabulary and Structure（词汇与结构 20%）

Directions: In this part there are 20 incomplete sentences. For each sentence there are four choices marked A, B, C and D. Choose the ONE answer that best completes the sentence.

1. _____ did you go in car this morning?

 A. How far   B. How much far away

 C. How long   D. How much

2. It was _____ that he couldn't finish it alone.

 A. a so difficult work   B. a so difficult job

 C. such a difficult work   D. such a difficult job

3. Bill, along with the three other men, _____ to represent the union at the next meeting.

 A. are   B. was

 C. were   D. is

4. Neither the driver nor the passengers on the bus _____ during our drive across the mountains.

 A. was frightened   B. was frightening

 C. were frightened   D. were frightening

5. Two thirds of the surface of the world _____ with water.

 A. are covered   B. is covered

 C. was covered   D. were covered

6. Hardly had she finished the composition _____ the bell rang.

 A. then   B. than

 C. so   D. when

7. So badly _____ in the accident that he had to stay in the hospital for a few weeks.

 A. did he injure   B. he did injure

 C. was he injured   D. he was injured

8. The faster we get this assignment done, _____ we can go out and play.

 A. soon   B. sooner

 C. that soon   D. the sooner

9. Her government insisted that she _____ until she finished her degree.

 A. stayed   B. stay

 C. would stay   D. shall stay

10. She apologized for _____ the party.

 A. not her being able to attend   B. her not being able to attend

 C. her being able not to attend   D. her being not able to attend

11. _____, the inhabitants fled.

    A. The city to take

    B. The city having been taken

    C. Having taken the city

    D. Taking the city

12. Everybody in the class must hand in _____ text paper within the given time.

    A. their

    B. our

    C. his

    D. her

13. The Nazi kept those _____ in their concentration camp.

    A. prisoner of war

    B. prisoners of war

    C. prisoner of wars

    D. prisoners of wars

14. Without the instrument, we _____.

    A. cannot hardly do nothing

    B. cannot hardly do anything

    C. can hardly do nothing

    D. can hardly do anything

15. I would like _____ if I am not prevented.

    A. to come

    B. come

    C. coming

    D. to have come

16. They appear _____ their tour to the island.

    A. enjoy

    B. enjoying

    C. to have been enjoyed

    D. to have enjoyed

17. Only by diligence and honesty _____.

    A. one can succeed in life

    B. can one succeed in life

    C. one can be succeeded in life

    D. can one be succeeded in life

18. The packet of chocolate was _____ the reach of the child.

    A. without

    B. under

    C. within

    D. behind

19. The house _____ by the wind.

    A. blew down

    B. was blown down

    C. was to blow down

    D. was blowed down

20. She doesn't like _____ indoors.

    A. to keep

    B. being kept

    C. to be keeping

    D. be kept

IV. Cloze Test (完形填空 20%)

Directions: There are 20 blanks in the following passage, and for each blank there are four choices marked A, B, C and D at the end of the passage. You should choose the ONE answer that best fits into the passage.

Bobby Adams was very __1__ as Dr. Smith examined him. The doctor looked __2__ the boy's throat, __3__ his temperature and listened to his heart. Finally, he asked Bobby's mother a few questions.

"When did Bobby begin ___4___ ill?"

"This morning when he ___5___. He said he ___6___ to go to school today."

"What did he eat ___7___ breakfast?"

"He ___8___ orange juice, two pieces of buttered toast, dry cereal, and milk."

"I see," The doctor asked Bobby, "How do you ___9___ now, my boy?"

Bobby answered, "Terrible. I think I ___10___."

The doctor said, "You ___11___. In fact, you'll be fine ___12___ dinner time."

"Oh, Doctor. Do you really think so?" Bobby's mother ___13___ very glad.

Dr. Smith answered, "Mrs. Adams, your son has a sickness that is very common ___14___ boys at a time ___15___. It comes and goes very ___16___."

Mrs. Adams said, "But I don't understand."

"Today," the doctor told her, "the most important baseball game of the year ___17___ television. If Bobby feels well ___18___ watch television this afternoon, and I think he ___19___, he will be fine when the game is finished. It's the only ___20___ I know for this sickness. Now, If you'll excuse me, I must go across the street to see the Morton's boy, Alfred. He seems to have the same thing Bobby has today."

1. A. quit   B. quiet   C. quite   D. quietly

2. A. into   B. for   C. at   D. through

3. A. took   B. measured   C. counted   D. decided

4. A. to be feeling   B. to feel   C. to be felt   D. feel

5. A. gets up   B. is getting   C. was getting up   D. got up

6. A. won't want   B. wants   C. felt too sick   D. doesn't want

7. A. for   B. at   C. during   D. in

8. A. ate   B. took   C. had   D. made

9. A. look like   B. seem   C. do   D. feel

10. A. am dying   B. am going to die C. must be dead   D. must be died

11. A. won't die   B. must not die   C. won't be dead   D. won't be died

12. A. at   B. by   C. in   D. on

13. A. looked   B. seemed   C. looks   D. seems

14. A. for   B. to   C. of   D. about

15. A. as it   B. as this   C. like it   D. like this

16. A. fast   B. quickly   C. soon   D. rapidly

17. A. is in   B. will be at   C. is on   D. is at

18. A. enough to   B. to   C. sufficiently to D. so as to

19. A. is   B. does   C. will   D. would

20. A. way   B. method   C. cure   D. treatment

V. Mistake Identification (挑错练习 10%)

Directions: Each of the following sentences has four underlined parts marked A, B, C and D. Identify the one that is NOT correct.

1. My roommate lives in a small town in central Missouri, a quiet town, which I would
                                                                A   B
   like to live myself.
        C   D

2. The United States is composed of fifty states, two of that are separated from the others
                            A   B   C   D
   by land or water.

3. The detectives were finally able to arrest the man who finger prints had been found on
                      A   B   C   D
   the table.

4. This course, that is a prerequisite for microbiology, is so difficult that I would rather
                  A   B   C
   drop it.
    D

5. Dr. Harder, which is the professor for this class, will be absent this week because of
                A   B   C   D
   illness.

6. The teacher tried to make the classes enjoyable that the students would take a greater
                A   B   C
   interest in the subject.
          D

7. On high mountains the air pressure is very low that the water will boil at a temperature
   A   B   C   D
   below 100℃.

8. The columnist feels sure who wins the election will have the support of the parties.
                A   B   C   D

9. The students were all industrious and did that the teacher had told them to do.
                      A   B   C   D

10. The reason for my return is because I forgot my keys.

      A   B   C   D

VI. Translation (翻译 20%)

1. Translate the following sentences into English (汉译英):

1) 我喜欢上网，但是恐怕它占用我太多时间。

2) 两个词之间没有差别，我真的不知道该选哪个。

3) 孩子们必须在六点前返回学校。

4) 直到最后一天詹姆斯才想出了这个主意。

5) 英文报纸拥有世界上最大的阅读人群。

2. Translate the following sentences into Chinese (英译汉):

1) People usually use their own special words to show their thoughts and feelings.

2) For some of us, though making friends is not difficult, we may not want to make the first move.

3) But most importantly of all, remember you play not only for money, but also for fun and your health.

4) Most of all, try to think about why your parents do this or do that.

5) There are a few differences between our schools today and schools fifty years ago.

VII. Writing (写作 5%)

Directions: You are required to write a letter of reply according to the following instructions given in Chinese.

说明：根据下面提供的信息写一封回信。

发信人：张强

收信人：美国 Vesta 公司的 Mr. Johnson

内容：本酒店在 5 月 10 日至 15 日可以提供 10 间双人间，全部位于 28 层，价格为 128 美元/天，包括免费早餐。如果要求房价 8 折优惠，则不包括免费早餐。对你们的咨询表示感谢，欢迎光临。

Key to Test One

I. Dialogue Completion (5%)

1. B	2. A	3. C	4. B	5. A

II. Reading Comprehension (20%)

1. B	2. A	3. B	4. D	5. C
6. A	7. C	8. C	9. B	10. A
11. D	12. A	13. B	14. B	15. A
16. C	17. B	18. C	19. C	20. C

III. Vocabulary and Structure (20%)

1. D	2. D	3. C	4. B	5. C
6. C	7. D	8. D	9. A	10. A
11. A	12. C	13. B	14. B	15. D
16. C	17. D	18. B	19. B	20. C

IV. Cloze Test (20%)

1. B	2. A	3. D	4. C	5. D
6. B	7. C	8. B	9. A	10. B
11. C	12. D	13. A	14. D	15. A
16. A	17. C	18. B	19. A	20. B

V. Mistake Identification (10%)

1. C	2. C	3. B	4. B	5. B
6. C	7. B	8. B	9. C	10. A

VI. Translation (10%)

1. 1) Emily met a famous singer at the gifts shop last week.

   2) Tina stayed together with her friends on the last school trip.

   3) Our class was divided into three groups.

   4) They used to play basketball after school.

   5) She is crazy about love stories.

2. 1) 教育不是目的，而是达到目的的手段。

2) 换言之，我们并非仅仅为了教育孩子而教育孩子。

3) 我们的目的是使他们能适应生活。

4) 生活是多样化的；教育也是如此。

5) 只要我们意识到这一点，我们就能明白，选择适当的教育体制至关重要。

VII. Writing (5%)

Notice

All professors and associate professors are requested to meet on time in the college conference room at 2:00 p.m. on April 18th, next Monday, to discuss questions of international academic exchanges.

College Office

April 11th, 2007

Key to Test Two

I. Dialogue Completion (5%)

1. B	2. D	3. D	4. A	5. C

II. Reading Comprehension (20%)

1. A	2. C	3. B	4. C	5. A
6. A	7. A	8. B	9. A	10. C
11. D	12. A	13. C	14. A	15. B
16. D	17. A	18. B	19. C	20. C

III. Vocabulary and Structure (20%)

1. B	2. A	3. B	4. C	5. B
6. C	7. A	8. A	9. C	10. B
11. A	12. C	13. A	14. B	15. C
16. D	17. C	18. A	19. A	20. B

IV. Cloze Test (20%)

1. C	2. D	3. C	4. B	5. A
6. D	7. B	8. C	9. B	10. D
11. A	12. D	13. C	14. C	15. A
16. A	17. C	18. D	19. B	20. D

V. Mistake Identification (10%)

1. D	2. B	3. C	4. A	5. A
6. D	7. D	8. B	9. B	10. C

VI. Translation (20%)

1. 1) The boys spent the whole morning discussing answers to the question.

2) Man is the only creature that can speak.

3) There is no creature that does not need sleep every day.

4) A good way to pass an exam is to work hard every day.

5) Don't forget to lock the door when you leave.

2. 1) 孩子们学习语言时，除了学词汇，还要学语法。

2) 事实上，他是当时他们国家最成功的作家之一。

3) 如果你自己都迟到了，就别指望她准时。

4) 我朋友和我都想去听音乐会，但我们二人都没有票。

5) 在西进运动中铁路起到了至关重要的作用。

VII. Writing (5%)

To: Mr. White

From: Helena (Secretary)

Time: 10 A.M., February 25th, 2007

Message: Mr. Johnson of Honeywell Co. called to say that he will leave for Beijing on business tomorrow, and won't be back until the end of the month. He wishes to cancel his appointment with you on the morning of the 30th this month. He will contact you for another appointment when he is back.

Key to Test Three

I. Dialogue Completion (5%)

1. A	2. D	3. C	4. A	5. D

II. Reading Comprehension (20%)

1. C	2. C	3. B	4. C	5. B
6. C	7. B	8. D	9. A	10. D
11. A	12. A	13. A	14. D	15. D
16. D	17. C	18. B	19. B	20. B

III. Vocabulary and Structure (20%)

1. A	2. D	3. D	4. C	5. B
6. D	7. C	8. D	9. B	10. B
11. B	12. C	13. B	14. D	15. A
16. D	17. B	18. C	19. B	20. B

IV. Cloze Test (20%)

1. B	2. C	3. A	4. B	5. C
6. C	7. A	8. C	9. D	10. B
11. A	12. B	13. B	14. B	15. D
16. B	17. C	18. A	19. C	20. C

V. Mistake Identification (10%)

1. B	2. B	3. C	4. A	5. A
6. B	7. B	8. B	9. B	10. D

VI. Translation (20%)

1. 1) I enjoy surfing the Internet, but it takes up too much of my time, I am afraid.

2) There's no difference between the two words. I really don't know which one to choose.

3) The boys must return to school by six o'clock.

4) It was on the very last day that James came up with this idea.

5) Newspapers in English today have the largest number of readers in the world.

2. 1) 人们经常用他们自己特有的词语来表示他们的想法和情感。

   2) 对我们有些人来说，交朋友并不难，难在我们不太愿意自己先迈出第一步。

   3) 最重要的是，你要记住你踢球是为了娱乐和健康，而不仅是为了赚钱。

   4) 首先想一想父母为什么做这做那。

   5) 我们现在的学校和五十年前的学校相比有些不同。

VII. Writing (5%)

April 25th, 2007
Vesta Corporation of the US

Dear Mr. Johnson,
Thank you very much for your inquiry about our hotel. We can offer 10 double rooms from 10th to 15th of May, and all of them are located on the 28th floor. The price of each room is $128 per day, including free breakfast. If a 20% discount is wanted, we'll not provide breakfast free of charge.

We are looking forward to seeing you in our hotel.

Yours sincerely,
Zhang Qiang